James H. Graff, Charles Henry Ross, Archibald Chasemore

The Twopenny Twins

A Domestic Drama for Home Reading

James H. Graff, Charles Henry Ross, Archibald Chasemore

The Twopenny Twins
A Domestic Drama for Home Reading

ISBN/EAN: 9783337258535

Printed in Europe, USA, Canada, Australia, Japan

Cover: Foto ©Andreas Hilbeck / pixelio.de

More available books at **www.hansebooks.com**

THE TWOPENNY TWINS.

A DOMESTIC DRAMA FOR HOME READING.

PERFORMED BY

MAJOR PENNY,

AND A NUMEROUS STAFF OF AUXILIARIES.

AND PUT ON THE STAGE BY

CHARLES H. ROSS.

THE SCENERY AND COSTUMES BY A. CHASEMORE,

THE MUSIC BY THE TWINS THEMSELVES.

"Twin-kle, twin-kle."—*Poem.*

LONDON:

"JUDY" OFFICE, 73 FLEET STREET, E.C.

INTRODUCTORY.

LADIES AND GENTLEMEN,—

THE MAJOR!

CONTENTS.

		PAGE
1.	THE TWINS HAPPEN	13
2.	THE TWINS WIDE AWAKE	17
3.	THE BLUEBOTTLE BUSINESS	22
4.	THE MAJOR PUTS SOMETHING IN HIS POCKET	28
5.	THE MAJOR TAKES SOMETHING OUT	34
6.	CHAOS PREVAILS	38
7.	MORE UNPLEASANTNESS	43
8.	TOOTSY GOES IT	45
9.	THE MAJOR SUFFERS	51
10.	THE SOOTHING SYSTEM	58
11.	FAILURE OF THE SOOTHING SYSTEM	63
12.	THE CHARMING GIRLS	69
13.	THE MAJOR HAS DOUBTS	74
14.	THE YOUNG LADIES CARRY ALL BEFORE THEM	78
15.	SOMETHING IS KNOCKED DOWN TO THE MAJOR	81
16.	NOTHING COULD BE NICER	86
17.	THE BOLD SOLDIER	93
18.	TEA AND A LITTLE MUSIC	99
19.	SOMETHING WRONG AGAIN	105
20.	THE TWINS NAMELESS	108
21.	NEARLY A TRAGEDY	116
22.	WHERE IS THERE A GODFATHER?	121
23.	THE GODFATHER LANDED	125
24.	THE CEREMONY	131
25.	THE TWINS' TEETH	138
26.	THE TWINS CAUSE ANXIETY	143
27.	SOMEBODY DOES SOMETHING SILLY	147
28.	TWOPENNY TURNS UP	151

CHAPTER I.

IN WHICH THE TWINS FIRST HAPPEN UNEXPECTEDLY.

AM Major Penny, the head of our family
We are four in number, and the others ar
girls. The Girls are of mature age. I an
forty-two.

Originally we were five in number. The fifth (wh
is now no more) gave us a great deal of trouble.
live in the country, at what some people might call aı
out-of-the-way place. The Girls live with me, and
manage all business matters connected with our estab
lishment and order the dinners.

The three surviving girls, my sisters, are namec
respectively Bathsheba, Cassandra, and Ursula, whicl
to some extent balances the Penny. As I am univer
sally addressed in the home circle, and elsewhere, a
the Major, my own Christian name is immaterial fo
the purposes of this narrative.

The fifth (who is now no more) was a Jemima. It was settled from the first that it would have been unreasonable to expect much of a Jemima—and we didn't. If No. 5 systematically persisted in being a surprise to the rest of her family, it is not her family's fault. The last surprise No. 5 (now no more) has given us has taken the shape of Twins.

Up to the last moment allowable before going to press, we have not got over them ; indeed, I may almost go as far as to say that the twins go on astonishing us more and more, and appear likely to do so.

Relative to previous surprises, and before dealing with the Twin episode, it may not be out of place here to say a few words. No. 5 was the only married member of our family. I am myself a bachelor. During their youth the Girls, like other girls, were come after from time to time ; but on all occasions I disapproved of the persons who did the coming-after-ing, and spoke my sentiments on the subject to the Girls. " Bathsheba, Cassandra, or Ursula " (as the case may be), I would observe, " the man is a Fool, an Idiot, and an Ass, and you must be a Confounded Donkey to care about him."

There is nothing, in a case of this kind, like putting the thing properly. Almost invariably the truth thus put came right home to the Girl's mind, and she saw I was right. The truth, in like manner, brought home to the young man was, as a rule, equally efficacious. In the case of hesitation on either side, I boxed the Girl's ears, and broke the young man's head, respectively. I have never known this to fail. Try it in your own family circle.

And it would not have failed in the case of No. 5 if it had been tried. For the case of No. 5, however, I was to a great extent unprepared. I did not—nor indeed did the other Girls, but that matters little— deem it at all probable that there would be any coming-after with regard to No. 5, called Jemima (now no more), and when we heard that she had not only been come after without our noticing it, but had been carried right off without our observing it till some time after it had occurred, we were, for the first time, seriously surprised.

When, presently, we got a letter mentioning the fact in a casual kind of way, amongst other particulars relating to the weather and scenery in the part of the world she and the young man were taking their honey-moon in, it staggered us for a while, and then I called for my pistols. The Girls, flinging themselves upon me and clinging to me wildly, coupled with the fact that I had no pistols at the time, happily tended to avoid the shedding of blood, and the carrier-off of No. 5 still lived—indeed, he lives now.

The next severe surprise was the revelation of the man's name, which we took at first to be a deliberate insult, until Bathsheba turned Twopenny up in the "Post-Office Directory." The fact established that there were absolutely Twopennys existing, in addition to the Pennys we were already aware of, we could not help feeling the fact itself was a kind of slur on us, and that Jemima, had she changed her name at all, ought not to have changed it to the disparagement of her own family.

We naturally felt that if any change had been

necessary, Jemima might have got out of copper coin-age, and been a Mrs. Silver, a Mrs. Shilling, or, indeed a Mrs. Pound; but, as has been already observed, we never expected anything at all satisfactory from Jemima.

Within a year the last thing but one anybody expected took place. Jemima quarrelled with her husband, left him, and sought shelter with the Girls and me. Before we had recovered from the shock which this event occasioned, came the last and most surprising of the surprises—the Twins.

At the present moment the Girls and I have the sole care of the twins, for, as I previously observed, their mother is no more. The twins are squeaking with all the strength of which they are capable. I am engaged in looking up the word "Infant," after failing to find "Baby," in the "Encyclopædia Britannica," for the purpose of ascertaining the best modes of treatment, whilst the Girls are discussing the relative merits of beef-tea and calves'-foot jelly.

I myself have doubts whether the twins are old enough—they were born only a week ago—for such treatment. The first nurse who attended the twins' mother Jemima (now no more) in her last illness, and had sole charge of the twin tribe up to now, has left us in a huff, owing to my giving her a bit of my mind; and if the ailments of early infancy are not fully treated in the "Encyclopædia Britannica," I shall feel uneasy.

CHAPTER II.

IN WHICH THE TWINS ARE WIDE AWAKE AND KICKING.

IT was a common remark with a late illustrious commander-in-chief that I, Major Penny, was the best man he ever knew at strategic movements with heavy artillery. Yet where am I now?

When I mention the fact that I am alone in the house with the twins, and that the twins are on the full howl, I may, perhaps, be more clearly understood and sympathized with should I repeat the question— Where am I now?

Upon the field of battle, whilst temporarily in command, I may have so disposed the men under me as to render highly valuable service. I will not deny it —and, indeed, why should I?—but here, in strict confidence, I own, in answer to the above interrogatory, I am rather worse than nowhere.

To some extent it may have been my fault that I am placed in the position in which I find myself. I may have been, to a certain extent, wrong in sending Ursula in search of What's-her-name's Soothing Syrup, when Bathsheba had just gone by my directions for Fennings' Powders, I having forgotten to add them to Cassandra's list, with the extra feeding-bottle, etcetera, which I had packed her off to fetch in advance of the other two Girls.

I have said that the twins are howling—but I anticipate. Let us rather go back a few minutes, and imagine the twins peacefully slumbering side by side.

Just at this instant it is rather difficult to imagine anything approaching such a state of things on the part of the twins, but let us try to do so.

The door, then, has just closed (with a bang) behind Ursula, and a moment afterwards I become conscious of a twitching in the off eyebrow of the near twin.

I hold my breath and wait. I am in the act of walking at the time: one leg is on the ground and the other isn't, when I become, as it were, frozen into stone, like the flying Mercury of ancient sculpture.

When, at last, I can't stand this way any longer without a fear of tumbling over, I bring down the other foot, and my boot creaks like anything.

On this the near twin puckers up its nose and sniffs. I immediately become transfixed again, and suffer agonies of suspense whilst I watch the puckers straighten out. Then I breathe again, and going in for extra cautiousness, kick the table.

At the noise the four eyes of the twin division open simultaneously, as though worked on one wire, and rivet themselves on my face, stretched across the table towards them, and wearing an expression of such con-centrated agony, rage, and despair, that it is quite too much for the twins, and the lines of their youthful countenances spread out perpendicularly, like the gutta-percha heads you buy at the corner shop in the Lowther, when you pinch them under the chin.

The next moment I am chanting, "Hush-a-bye baby, have you any wool? Father's gone a-hunting on a tree-top!" in a persuasive tone of voice, whilst I flip the fingers of my right hand as an accompaniment, and rub my shin with the left.

These must be fools of twins, as far as music is concerned!—they don't see it.

I therefore rock them in their little cot, and jolt one twin's head up against the other with a rattling sound, like eggs going at a trot in a basket to market. But even this does not soothe them.

Under these circumstances, I come to the conclusion they will, perhaps, calm down if carried about a bit; but it is a harder thing to carry a couple of twins, both

"In arms."

together, than any one who has never carried half a twins at a time has any notion of, and the way I hold them gives them an opportunity of pulling and hauling at my whiskers in a style I have been unaccustomed to.

There was a time, during the Crimean War, when a

Russian officer, whom I subsequently slew, expressed a desire to take me by the nose, but probably that was not a case in point. As it is, I am now being similarly assaulted, and have also had a dab in either eye. Indeed, the question is, What will happen next? unless——I'll try the feeding-bottle.

Hitherto we have only got one feeding-bottle between the twins—naturally supposing that they would have taken their food fairly and squarely turn about—but they won't. When one twin gets the bottle the other howls, and there's no way of choking off the howler but by gagging him with the india-rubber feeder, on which the other fellow pipes up like one o'clock.

"Aha! the bottle!"

It is the case now; but whilst No. 1 twin is wolfing up his share, I shake a rattle with all my might in the face of No. 2, which has the effect of stunning him a bit till his turn comes, when I rattle up the other chap till he seems half dazed.

After these proceedings, both twins being temporarily lulled, I get them back into their cot, and unbutton my waistcoat and gasp awhile.

They continue quiet. If I could open the window and get a breath of air, I might go on looking up the ills of infancy in the " Encyclopædia " with some degree of calmness.

The twins have closed their eyes. I will......gently ......That's right......And now for the " Encyclopædia."

I suppose the Girls will be back soon. Really and truly, I am not getting on so very badly ; but, after all, tact is what is wanted in these matters—simply tact......What's that ?

A beast of a big buzzing bluebottle fly has come in through the open window.

" Singularly incomplete, this work."

I watch this bluebottle with interest. As I supposed, he goes for the twins.

He settles on the off twin's nose. The off twin lunges out at him, and he beats a retreat.

The off twin sinks back into slumber. Heaven be thanked!

The bluebottle returns and settles on the near twin's nose. The near twin lunges, and gives his brother one in the ear. On this, the off twin lunges out and howls.

I oblige with "Cease, rude Boreas," and "The Red, White, and Blue," and peace is restored.

Then I look round for the bluebottle. He is quiet just now, but I'm not going to put up with any of his nonsense. Let him look out.

Aha!

He returns and hovers playfully round his victims. Which nose is he on for now? Let him look out!

Whilst I fix my gentleman with my eye, I take out my silk handkerchief, and at a critical moment I flip.

Merciful powers! what have I done? Have I marked a twin for life? And which was it?

They are both howling at the top of their voices.

CHAPTER III.

IN WHICH THE MAJOR HAS IT OUT WITH THE BLUEBOTTLE.

IT may here be casually mentioned that I (Major

Penny), during the Indian Revolt, was the first person
to whom the notion of blowing Sepoys from the
mouths of guns first occurred. Others may have gone

Rage and fury.

about taking the credit, but it was I (Major Penny)
who said right off before anybody, " Blow 'em to
smithereens!   The only way to quell the mutiny is to
blow 'em to smithereens."

I do not exactly quote the above as a case in point ;
it is more with a view to showing that when a mutiny
is in question, and you want a queller, you might do
worse than send for yours obediently.

    *   *   *   *   *   *

To begin with, I am naturally anxious to ascertain
whether I really did flick a bit off one of the twins'
noses when aiming at the bluebottle, but a careful in-
vestigation proves this impression to have been errone-

ous.   On the whole, I am not sorry that it is not so—
not only on the twins' account, but because it would
have been deuced awkward to have satisfactorily
accounted for the circumstance on the Girls' return.

Without going lengthily into detail, I may observe
that the circumstance might have tended to lower my
system of quelling in the Girls' eyes.

As it is, seeing that I expect either Bathsheba, Cassandra, or Ursula to return immediately, it is necessary
that the twins should be silenced at once, and the
only question that remains to be answered is, How?

I observe that inordinate gluttony is the besetting
sin of both twins alike, and once more I deem it advisable to allow them an opportunity, as Mr. Cruikshank
would say, to "console themselves with the bottle."

The fact that there is but one bottle between them
acts prejudicially in this instance, and whilst the lucky
one pulls away with an expression on him resembling
a Highland piper discoursing his national music, envy
and uncharitableness goads the other twin well-nigh
to frenzy, and he claws, in a futile fashion, at the
coveted object, and bewails his paplessness in the
shrillest treble.

I therefore vary the monotony by letting twin No. 2
have a pull, and endeavour to lull No. 1's suspicion of
foul play by substituting my thumb in the place of the
sucker, at which, thinking no guile, he wires in for a
period, and is perfectly contented.

Whilst occupied by this strategic movement, it
occurs to me that my position, viewed by an unsym-
pathetic stranger, might appear somewhat undignified.

"Major Penny," I mentally ejaculate, "you who have

led men to action—who have stormed giddy heights amidst blinding fire, and have hacked your way through forests of deadly steel—to what occupation have you come at last? Major Penny, if any one should catch a glimpse of you under present circumstances, he would smile."

But, on second thoughts, how poor and paltry would be his triumph! Did not the great Alfred unbend to bake cakes and burn them? Did not.........

No. 1 twin is beginning to notice a want of something in the substitute I have provided. He had better have the bottle again, and his brother take a pull at the other thumb.

So! The exchange has been swiftly effected. General joy at present prevails. Both twins are peaceful now. Sleep, sweet sleep, steals gently o'er their senses. I'm getting the cramp with stooping, but no matter.

*   *   *   *   *   *

I have done it. I have withdrawn my thumb with a slow and cautious movement, leaving a round hole where it has been, but the unconscious twin slumbers placidly

After all, there are many kinds of victories. There is the victory of the diplomatist. There is—— *That confounded bluebottle come back again!*

I thought so! Would you? No, you don't!

He is making straight for the noses of my young friends, but I am too quick for him.

He retreats, and I follow on his trail, like Mr. Fenimore Cooper's Chingaghook (whose name, I trust, I am spelling properly).

He makes a tour of the room, on finding that he
cannot effect his purpose, and lodges on the mantel-
piece. I do the Chingaghook business.

He is in my power! Aha!

I 've missed him!

He makes another tour of the apartment, pretend-
ing he doesn't know I 'm in it. Let him beware!
This trifling is ill-timed.

Here he is alighting on a side-table. I repeat the
Chingaghookery

With bated breath I take a deadly aim!

Destruction.

He 's up again, and I am following in hot pursuit.
Crash!!!

I had not noticed another side-table whilst urging
on my wild career—a table littered over with Bath-
. sheba's confounded old china cups and saucers.

I bear down on them like an avalanche, and in

another moment fell destruction has been wrought, and I am sprawling amongst the ruins.

I get up and gaze upon the field of battle. I collect scraps and hold them together, hoping they will stick by magic, whilst I reflect on the state of mind Bathsheba will be in when she finds out what has happened, and the trouble I shall have in framing a dignified explanation of the business, unless——

No, that were unmanly ; and, besides, I don't think it would be believed. I *cannot* lay it on the twins.

Meditation.

The twins, it may be mentioned, have been awakened by the noise, and are now howling again as hard as ever.

Meanwhile the brute of a bluebottle is buzzing away joyously, and——

Rat-a-tat-tat-a-tat-tat !

A knock at the door! The Girls returned, no doubt.

Deception.

Which? Probably Bathsheba; and, as yet, I have not
a word ready in the way of explanation.

Supposing, to gain time, I pocket the bits.

I have.   Now for it!

---o---

CHAPTER IV.

IN WHICH THE MAJOR PUTS SOMETHING IN HIS COAT-TAIL POCKET.

Good gracious!

It is not my sister Bathsheba, as I at first supposed,
or one of the other Girls.   It is neither more nor less
than Lady Taltorkington, of Taltorkington Towers,
one of the leading qualities of the neighbourhood,

whose carriage stands without, and whose footman has knocked till he was tired, when Lady Taltorkington herself has taken her turn, and has the knocker in her hand when I drag the door open suddenly, and as nearly as possible throw her on her nose in the passage.

"Hallo !"

Next moment I am apologizing profusely, and trying to hide the feeding-bottle with one hand, whilst I offer the other to her ladyship to shake.

Her ladyship seems a little taken aback, on the whole, but yet smiles sweetly and asks after the Girls, on which, to carry off the detail of the bottle, the india-rubber tubing to which persists in wagging to and fro, behind me, like the pendulum of a clock, I rush into uncalled-for particulars, and give a history of the Girls' ailments for the last month or two.

I also beg and entreat of her to come in, as though

it were a matter of life or death to me that she should, praying in my heart all the while that she won't. It is needless to say she does, and settles into a seat, as though for years.

By a sleight-of-hand trick, which I honestly believe

"So glad!"

to be superior to anything ever attempted by Messrs. Maskelyne and Cooke, I get the bottle away behind a work-box on the top of the new piano Cassandra is buying on the hire system, and glide gracefully into a chair opposite her ladyship.

Crack!

*   *   *   *   *   *

Instinctively I should have known by the sound even, if not by sensations of not too pleasurable a nature, that the tea-pot was continuing to come to sorrow in consequence of my sitting on it; but it will perhaps call attention unnecessarily to the circumstances if I alter my position.

Crack !

It has gone off again of its own accord, without any additional movement on my part, but I continue to dilate on Ursula's toothache without a pause.

Her ladyship does not appear to follow me. She, on the contrary, looks as though the noise puzzled her.

She says, " What ever was that ? "

I say "What was what ?" as naturally as possible, and break a little more china turning. Then, thinking it best at this juncture to appear to look as though I were trying to hear something, although I had heard nothing hitherto, I add, " Hush ! what can it be ? "

The guilty conscience.

A deathlike silence of one moment ensues, as all the china breakable has been broken by this time, and then next moment another sound of a most mysterious character is audible.

On hearing it, Lady Taltorkington appears to prick up her ears, and I too am singularly interested. It is, in fact, a sound as of the dripping of water blended

with subdued music partaking of the nature of the
Æolian harp.

When I thoroughly realize that it is the contents of
the twins' feeding-bottle dripping steadily down among
the machinery of Cassandra's piano on the hire system, I writhe covertly, and use (inaudible) bad language.

With a mental effort equal to several Talleyrands
under high pressure, I observe, " The rain on the roof
of the conservatory."

" It 's just like a baby ! "

Her ladyship shakes her head dubiously.   " I don't
hear it now at all," she says.

Thank goodness ! Who wanted her to ? Suddenly,
however, she starts.

" It 's just like a baby ! " she exclaims.   " How extraordinary ! "

As she speaks, I for the first time become conscious
of the piping (bagpiping rather) music peculiar to
those ghastly twins, for one of whom, probably, the

bluebottle is just now making it warm, without fear of interference.

But how is it possible to tell the truth to her lady-ship without telling the humiliating story in its entirety of that unhappy woman Twopenny's injudicious mar-riage and ill-advised twin legacy?

I therefore dissemble. I say,

"Baby! Good gracious! What an idea!"

Immediately on making this observation the other twin joins in the harmony, and the two pleasant young voices swell the chorus.

Once, however, having strayed from the path of strict veracity, I find myself engulfed in a vortex of untruthfulness, as it were, and plunge wildly into the weather, and talk of yesterday's glorious sunshine as something wholly unprecedented in the experience of man.

In the course of time, finding I have worked out the sunshine topic, which, after all, as a topic, has not been much of a success, I am turning over in my mind whether Cassandra's nettle-rash last autumn, or the atrocities in Bulgaria, would go best as a follower, when a loud bump on the floor of the next room brings me to a full stop.

Hallo!

What has happened now? The twins can't have got up, and by their united efforts upset another table?

A deathlike silence follows the bump in the next room. It is the sort of silence which holds you spell-bound when you are sitting for your photograph; during which you think over all the incidents of your

early life, as people say a man does who is on the point
of drowning.

There is a deathlike silence in this room also, broken
but by one faint sound—the steady drip from the
twins' bottle into the interior of the hire system.

This suspense is terrible. What is going to happen
next?

-----*o*-----

CHAPTER V

IN WHICH THE MAJOR TAKES SOMETHING OUT OF HIS POCKET.

WHEN I casually mention that I, Major Penny, have
in my time wallowed knee-deep in the gore of battle-
fields, it may surprise you to hear that, at this moment,
I find myself almost unnerved.

Whilst rushing to the breach amidst showers of
deadly lead, I own I have occasionally asked myself
with some curiosity what may be waiting for me
within. In heading a forlorn hope, indeed, the idea
not unfrequently suggests itself; yet, I repeat, that
that suspense is nothing to the suspense now.

This may possibly be accounted for to some extent
by the novelty of the situation. At the call of duty, in
foreign parts, I have in my time made short work of a
lot of blacks, without noticing that the exercise in any
way interfered with my appetite or my sleep; but if

anything has happened to one or both of those twins, I don't quite know what I shall do.

Extraordinary to relate, her ladyship appears not to notice my agitation. It is true that this may be owing to the fact of the twins having subsided into silence.

And this does not at first occur to me. To me the twins' silence is wholly unaccountable. If they are alive and awake, they ought to be on full pipe. I must and will know the worst.

I am rising to my feet with this intention, when her ladyship, laying her hand upon my arm, arrests my progress. She says,

"I see, Major, you agree with me, and I may rely on your support."

It would appear from this observation that her ladyship has been talking for some time past without my noticing the circumstance.

I have already told you, I believe, that Lady Taltorkington is one of the leading qualities of our neighbourhood. I may also add that it has been my one aim and object for years past to cultivate her acquaintance, to which statement I may also add that this is her first visit to my humble dwelling.

I wonder whether she will ever come again? Meanwhile, although I haven't a notion what the deuce she has been talking about, perhaps I had better say something.

I therefore smile cheerfully, and respond, "If my support is of any value, your ladyship may depend on me—to the utmost."

"I was sure I could, Major Penny," she says with

warmth, as she produces a note-book. "What shall we say?"

I don't quite follow this. It begins to look deucedly like a subscription.

I try to arouse myself, but am incapable of any mental effort, and instead listen intently for the slightest noise in the next room.

All is silence there. Her ladyship goes on tackling me.

"Come, Major," she says, "you mean to surprise us all, I can see. Three figures, eh?"

By all that's horrible, it *is* a subscription she is on to! And three figures! I like that.

I make a desperate effort to save myself, and say, "Let me understand, now, what is the exact nature of the—the proposition, as it stands."

Her ladyship looks surprised and slightly offended. "I thought I had fully explained," she says.

"Oh, perfectly," I hasten to reply. "I was only thinking whether, owing to certain circumstances which it would fatigue you to go into, I should be altogether justified in—in entering into the matter as I could wish, did I—I—only consult my own inclinations."

Considering that I had not the remotest notion what she had been talking about, I rather fancy this sentence is nicely turned.

"My dear Major," she says, "you astonish me. I had indeed relied upon your aid on the platform."

She wants to get me on a platform now. Next it will be a tight-rope, I suppose.

"Since, however, you will not take a personal part

I must, I presume, be content with your subscription. What shall I say?"

It *is* a subscription: that is quite plain now.

"I have so many calls upon me just at this moment, but if a guinea is of any service——"

"A guinea, Major!" she exclaims. "Oh, I had hoped for so much more!"

Confound her hopes! I think I'm sufficiently victimized as it is.

"But," she continues, "it is to be considered as a quarterly payment, of course. Shall I take it now?"

This is highway robbery, but I can't see my way out of it on easier terms, and I would do anything almost, just at this moment, to get rid of her.

The silence in the next room is tomb-like.

*   *   *   *   *   *

"Here's a go!"

Whew! She has gone, and my one pound one with her. Though the subject is a painful one, I can scarcely

refrain from a smile when I reflect on the way in which
I bestow my charity.   There is an open-handed vague-
ness abqut it that really is refreshing from its novelty.
But hush !   How about those twins ?

I hold my breath as I turn the handle of the door,
and glare affrightedly around.

It is as I half expected.   The worst has happened.

*The cradle is lying wrong side up, and the twins are
underneath.*

To the rescue !

CHAPTER VI.

IN WHICH CHAOS PREVAILS, AND THE GIRLS COME BACK AGAIN.

IN deadly terror I remove the cradle, the blankets,
the pillows, etcetera, and arrive at last at the twins.
They are lying on their little noses, motionless.

As I stretch forth my hand and seize them, I hear a footfall in the passage. The Girls returned, perhaps. Well, they had better know all—— The deuce!

    *   *   *   *   *   *

It isn't the Girls. It is that confounded woman come back again.

"Unhand me!"

"Major!"

"Unhand me!" I shriek, and rushing back, fling myself against the door.

By the way, I trust she won't think I'm mad!

There is no doubt about it.

She does think I am mad—probably dangerous.

She has flown from the house, and, looking after her, I see her gesticulating wildly to the coachman, and, seemingly, telling him of her narrow escape from the raging maniac!

Stay, though! Perhaps she knows the truth, and is on her way to the police-station. In a short time the myrmidons of the law may be here asking for explanations relative to the smothered babes——

Never!

Good gracious!

There's nothing at all smothered in that now welcome sound. They were actually only asleep, then,

Away—away!

all the time. And twins can, seemingly, slumber
wrong side up, and extinguished by a cradle. There
is yet something to learn in this world, even for a

Major who has headed a charge on the ensanguined field of battle.

Pipe up, my merry men! Don't mind how much row you make—pipe up!

Meanwhile, before the Girls come back, let me try to set things a little bit straight. At present, our usually orderly apartments wear something of the aspect of the stage of a theatre during the pantomime season after a pelting scene. The first thing is to

More mischief.

make sure there are no fragments of broken china lying about—or, stay, let me first look at the piano.

Confound this bottle! It is spoiling something else now. Inadvertently I have placed it on the top of one of Ursula's water-colour sketches. The deuce!

*   *   *   *   *   *

Evidently I have adopted a wrong system in trying to wipe it with my pocket-handkerchief. Here are

half a forest and the top of a mountain come off, and
the sea has run over the margin.

There'll be a row about this.

*   *   *   *   *   *

There is a row about it going on at this moment,
and some other rows about other little matters. The
Girls have come back in a body, and the first thing
Bathsheba's eye lit upon was a bit of her tea-pot, half
hidden under the leg of the table. Meanwhile Ursula
is weeping over her water-colours, and Cassandra, with
tears in her eyes, is polishing the top of her piano.
Luckily she does not know that anything has happened to the inside.

"Hallo!"

We are interrupted at this moment by a knock.
Of course it is the new nurse whom Ursula went to
inquire about, and who is to come on immediately,
and high time it is she did.

*   *   *   *   *   *

This is awkward! It is not the nurse. It is a young man come to tune the piano.

I dissemble whilst he raises the lid. But when I hear him say, "Hallo!" it occurs to me I might as well go for a constitutional, and I go.

  *   *   *   *   *   *

CHAPTER VII.

IN WHICH THERE IS MORE UNPLEASANTNESS.

I MUST confess, as I continue my walk, and the humble peasants I encounter by the way move on one side and respectfully salute me—I must confess I cannot refrain from asking myself whether I, Major Penny, who have led Her Majesty's forces (or, at any rate, a portion of them) to action, have not recently been placed in a somewhat undignified position.

It cannot be denied that the business of nursing (particularly in the case of twins) more naturally devolves upon a member of the other sex, whom it does not seem to worry quite so much, or, anyhow, they don't own to it.

I have been perusing this morning, with much pleasure, an account of the reading of a paper by Mrs. W. E. Gladstone, at the Domestic Economy Congress at Birmingham, in which the writer urged strongly that the elementary principles of nursing should be added to the subjects already taught in schools, so that they might become part of the regular instruction of young girls. A child might be so taught to nurse as to give her what was really a high and holy aim.

These are my sentiments too, and it is to be re-gretted that the Girls—Bathsheba, Cassandra, and Ursula—were not thus instructed when young.

The ribald scoffer might perchance suggest that,

At it again !

hitherto, they have not stood in any particular need of such knowledge, and that, in the ordinary course of events, they were by no means ever likely to.

But a truce to irrelevance. Afflicted as we are by twins requiring an abnormal amount of nursing, an experienced nurse is a *sine quâ non ;* and, from what I can learn, Mrs. Tootsy is the nurse of all nurses for us!

Indeed, from what has reached me, it would appear that Mrs. Tootsy would have been equal to triplets, and is reported to have said that she had been in a family with whom twins were a mere matter of periodical recurrence.

With the aid of so valuable a person, I feel that I can manage the two Twopennys without trouble.

As I approach the house on my return, all is calm. I let myself in quietly and look around. In the passage is a bandbox bearing the name of Tootsy.

Impelled by natural curiosity, I raise the lid, and discover a large black bottle, doubtless containing soothing cordial for the twins. I will taste it.

I have. It's gin!

At this moment the rustle of a skirt behind me attracts my attention, and a strange voice exclaims,

"What! you're at it again, are you?"

It is Mrs. Tootsy, who evidently does not know who I am.

CHAPTER VIII.

IN WHICH TOOTSY GOES IT.

I HAVE serious doubts with regard to the woman Tootsy.

To a certain extent I am willing to allow the woman Tootsy might have been justified in addressing an unknown person she found sipping out of her gin-bottle with some amount of abruptness.

The words, "You're at it again, are you?" although they might be taken to imply a foreknowledge on her part of my being in the habit of being at it whensoever an occasion offered, might not, however, necessarily mean quite as much. Considered as a mere ordinary figure of speech, the observation loses something of its offensiveness; yet, I repeat, I have serious doubts with regard to the woman Tootsy.

Does, or does not, the woman Tootsy look up to and respect me, as a person in her position ought to look up to and respect her employer?

I don't think it.

With all the sternness I can call into my features at a moment's notice, the spirits having taken a little of my breath away, I turn upon Tootsy, at the same time replacing the cork in the bottle, and ask whether the bottle is hers.

" It ain't yours, anyhow," says Tootsy.

There is truth in this, though it be blended with a certain amount of disrespect. I therefore say, with quiet dignity, " I do not dispute the fact, but I ask for further information."

" You hand it over, will you?" says Tootsy. " I don't know how long you've been at it, but there's a third gone!"

" If you intend to insinuate that I have taken——" I begin with what I trust is pardonable warmth, but she breaks in upon me.

She says, " Well, of all the barefaced! Why, I see you with my own eyes!"

I feel I am losing dignity if this goes on much longer, and must at once put matters on their proper footing. I therefore say,

" You do not appear to be aware, Mrs. Tootsy, that

you are addressing the master of this house. I—I am Major Penny!"

"I'm sure," says Mrs. Tootsy, with candour, "I didn't know who you was or who you wasn't, but I don't see what business you've got interfering with my things, and it's what I never did, and never will, put up with from any person alive!"

In making this declaration Mrs. Tootsy raises her voice, and the sound of it brings the Girls out into the passage.

As it is my custom to avoid personal altercations of any kind before the Girls, I deem it, at this point, politic to cut the argument short with an affable smile, and say, "Certainly, Mrs. Tootsy, it's all a mistake, so we won't say any more about it."

Mrs. Tootsy's face speaks volumes, but she happily remains silent, contenting herself by tipping up the bottle, and forming a close calculation of the quantity missing.

This conduct on the part of Tootsy is, I must own, anything but what it ought to be, and I have the strongest possible desire to then and there order her out of the house. But how can I do so without entering into details—and before the Girls that would be impossible.

Besides, this nurse has been too much trouble to get, for us to part lightly with her.

The only thing, then, left for me to do is, for the present, to curb my indignation and to bide my time.

Meanwhile Tootsy's behaviour continues to be trying. One of Tootsy's rules—and one that must be broken on no account—is, that Tootsy shall not be disturbed at her meals. Tootsy's meals are four per diem, with hot meat at each and bottled stout at two of them, and between whiles at irregular periods.

Tootsy's meal-time.

If the twins have convulsions during Tootsy's meals, it is of no consequence. She is not to be disturbed.

I have the misfortune to leave my hat and gloves in the room where she is dining, and don't dare to go in and fetch them.

Fortunately I am unobserved, so there is less loss of dignity about it ; but I sit on the bench in the hall three-quarters of an hour, waiting till Tootsy has quite done, before I can obtain possession of my property and go out for a walk.

In her treatment of the twins, Tootsy is, to my thinking, peculiar; but as I am informed, upon the best authority (Tootsy's own), that she is a woman of great experience, I am afraid to make a suggestion.

I can't help thinking, however, if the eldest twin is shaken up much more, something will be displaced in his youthful interior.

Again, although I own the twins' noses were a dis-

Tootsy's shake-up.

appointment to me when I first saw them—for ours is a family of noses with some character about them —I have doubts respecting the moulding process adopted by Tootsy.

According to Tootsy, you may put any shape you like upon a baby's nose, if you begin early enough, and tweak it hard and often enough in the required direction. If, in the case of these unhappy twins, Tootsy has taken the handle of Aldgate pump as her model, I think the noses already give great promise of resemblance.

But, of all things I have to complain of, I complain most of Tootsy's want of respect.

I have just been on a tour of inspection in the

4

nursery, and have made a few passing remarks, which have been received with snorts of defiance, in a low but determined tone.

I am now taking my afternoon constitutional, and

Tootsy's great nose trick.

observe some surprise in the expression of persons whom I encounter.

I wonder as I walk. Then presently a boy makes an unseemly remark in the rear of me. I turn quickly, and catch a glimpse of something white which turns with me. I turn again quickly, and the white thing turns quicker.

The boy laughs—other people laugh.

I get very hot and angry.

The mysterious something is beyond my reach.

I make a wild snatch at it. Good heavens! who has dared——

Gross indignity.

It is a duster, and it has been attached to my coat-tail by a pin!

As I occupy a position directly in the centre of the village high street, endeavouring to get hold of the confounded pin's head, molten fury fills my breast.

If this is Tootsy's work, let her look out.

———o———

CHAPTER IX.

IN WHICH THE MAJOR SUFFERS MUCH.

I HAVE one simple question to ask. Am I—Major Penny—master of my own house, or am I not master of my own house?

I don't know that there is any particular necessity
for me to pause for a reply. Rather let me reply myself by another question. If I am not master of my
own house, who the deuce is? Probably—and, at any
rate, apparently—the woman Tootsy.

Of course, I acknowledge that it was an absolute
necessity that the twins should have a proper nurse,
and I am also willing to admit that it is only fair that
the nurse should be allowed, to a great extent, full
power in her proper sphere—the nursery; but there
are limits to everything, even Tootsy, and Tootsy goes
beyond hers, and keeps on at it.

The woman Tootsy pervades the entire establishment. In the kitchen a perpetual civil war rages be-
twixt her and the cook, the partially smothered fury
of which reaches the upstairs rooms in gusts, as it
were, when the dining-room door opens for a moment
to allow of the passage of portions of our dinner.

The woman Tootsy, cook tells me, won't leave her
saucepans alone, and the truth of this statement has
already been twice exemplified by the substitution at
table of pap for bread sauce.

A tendency to coddling is possibly natural enough
in a nurse, but there are, on an average, on the simmer,
four saucepans, two jugs, and a kettle in the nursery
alone, besides one or two downstairs in the kitchen.

But this is not all. When the woman Tootsy first
came, I generously bade her order all that was necessary of our chemist and grocer. As the Girls and I
had not the remotest notion what might be necessary,
and did not want to be asked conundrums on the subject, I thought that that was the wisest course.

But the results are alarming. When I mention that I have, during a casual and clandestine glance round, become, for the first time, aware of the existence of two kinds of Infant Preservatives, and that infants may have a choice of food made by Hard, Neave, Nestle, Ridge, Savory & Moore, and about half a dozen others, and that the Twopenny Twins have

" *Can* this be good for twins ?"

alternate tucks-out at all of them, you may form some idea what the chemist and grocer's bills will be like this quarter, but I'll be hanged if I can!

And you may add to the packets of food, boxes of babies' powders innumerable, and everything in the way of soothing syrups and elixirs which the mind of man or woman ever conceived, or the stomach of infancy is capable of containing.

Gazing on these regiments of boxes and bottles, my eye alights on a formidable glass jar, on which the words Epsom Salts, in imposing capitals, arrest my attention, and I own I am staggered.

I do not profess to know everything about babies, though I have recently read up the subject to some considerable extent. But I protest against Epsom Salts being applied — and, apparently, in gigantic doses—to twins of so tender an age.

"It's rather strong

How, then, shall I proceed? At this moment I cannnot quite decide, and I hear Tootsy's step upon the stairs.

My first inclination is to heave the bottle through the open window, and scatter its fragments far and wide; my second, to escape with it to my own room, and that I do. Now I shall have time to settle a course of action for the future.

*　　*　　*　　*　　*　　*

I have always looked upon Epsom Salts as an admirable medicine, and it is one which I have been in the habit of taking periodically for years past; and that reminds me I am at present out of salts. There can surely be no great harm——

*   *   *   *   *   *

These are stronger salts than I have been in the habit of taking. Possibly they are Tootsy's private and particular, and being in the trade, as it were, she may have opportunities of obtaining her own private and particular, pure and unadulterated.—Bless me! what's that?

The gong for lunch. I had no idea it was lunch-time, or I should not have taken such a dose! And we've liver and bacon, too!—a dish to which I don't mind owning I am remarkably partial.

We are at lunch—the Girls and I—Bathsheba facing me, Cassandra on my right, Ursula on my left; the liver and bacon occupying the centre of the table. The Girls also are partial to the dish. They would not have it publicly spread about, of course; and at the dinner-table, were any one dining with us, the thing would be altogether out of the question; but here and now——

*   *   *   *   *   *

The Girls have all had a second help. I, too, am about——Good gracious!

There are shrill cries upon the landing. The woman Tootsy's voice is distinctly audible. She says some one has been at her bottles, and has taken away the oxalic acid!

There are moments in which we are said to live

years.   The moment I occupy looking for my hat is
one of them.

And the nearest stomach-pump is at the doctor's, a
mile off!

G-g-g-good gracious!

"Oh, dear! oh, dear! if any one's took it!"

Promptitude has ever been one of my most striking
characteristics.   I have shown it on the field of battle,
and I show it now.

The Girls scream in chorus, "For mercy's sake, say
what has happened!"   But I have no time for explanations.   What I have got to do is to run!

I run like mad!   I drop my hat.   I have not time
to pick it up.   The oxalic acid is commingling in a
lively fashion with the liver and bacon, and the effects
are terrible.

I accomplish half the distance, and am on the point
of sinking to the earth, when I descry the doctor in his
gig, and hail him frantically.

"G-g-g-good gracious!"

*   *   *   *   *   *

I have now been an inmate of the doctor's house for over an hour, and have taken strong emetics, and otherwise have had a time of it. The doctor is now going to bring what remains of me home in his gig.

*   *   *   *   *   *

On the doorstep an excited group. The Girls! They seem delighted about something. Bathsheba exclaims, "It's all right! It was a false alarm. Mrs. Tootsy has found the oxalic acid bottle in her cupboard, and nobody is a bit the worse!"

This is almost a joke in its way. But it might make me look ridiculous before the Girls if they knew what I had gone through.

I must beg of the doctor not to tell.

CHAPTER X.

IN WHICH THE MAJOR TRIES THE SOOTHING SYSTEM.

As from the circumstance of my not having previously referred to Dawkins you may possibly be unaware that there *is* a Dawkins in my establishment, I hasten to make a statement.

There is no doubt whatever as to Dawkins's existence, and if you lived in the same house, she would let you know it.

Dawkins.

Dawkins officiates as cook in my establishment, and she fills up her spare time as chambermaid and parlourmaid, as we only keep one servant. Dawkins's culinary feats are marvellous, though not in the sense you might suppose; and what is more marvellous still is the way in which the Girls and I have put up with them for years.

The impression upon the Girls' minds and mine is, that if Dawkins were to desert us, chaos would ensue as a matter of course, and Dawkins seems to share this opinion.

It is, therefore, Dawkins's habit periodically to come to the conclusion that she has been too long in the place, and that a change would be desirable ; and it is then our habit to conciliate her to the utmost in our power, and beg she won't think of it, to which at length she consents somewhat reluctantly, and we breathe again.

Dawkins having been with us a good long while, now knows our ways ; and this may also be said of us with respect to Dawkins's ways ; and we take particular care not to put her out of any of her ways, because, when she *is* put out, terrible things occur to the food.

When the Twins calamity first occured to us, Dawkins had to be conciliated like anything, but she has never yet got quite straight again. She was very nearly getting straight when Tootsy happened, but now it 's awful.

I take it Tootsy, hitherto, has been pretty well in the habit of having it all her own way wherever she has been ; but in Dawkins Tootsy has caught a Tartar, and war is waged and things broken all day long.

The one aim and end of Tootsy's existence, according to Dawkins, is to "mess up" basins; whilst, according to Tootsy, the one aim and end of Dawkins's is to chuck Tootsy's twin preparations in the dust-hole.

Whilst engaged with my private correspondence in my study, I require silence. My correspondence is somewhat one-sided, being chiefly devoted to the composition of letters to the "Times," of which I retain copies to be sent again, if—as is, I may say, invariably the case—the first one is not put in, or to be addressed to the editor of our local journal, who, though kept comparatively in the background by the exercise of hatred and malice, appears to me to possess powers of appreciation, conspicuous by their absence in other quarters.

The silence necessary for the exercise of the higher mental faculties called forth by this correspondence is, however, since the twins and Tootsy, almost wholly denied me. The fact of the room above being the twins' dormitory may account for the perpetual rocking of the cradle at such times as Tootsy is not engaged in pacing the length and breadth of the apartment like a wild beast in its cage, or at such other times as the twins, during Tootsy's absence (probably to mess up basins in the kitchen), are not on full cry.

Giving up the study as the very last place in the world suitable to study in, I take my pen and ink and paper into the drawing-room, and request the Girls, as a particular favour, to leave off chatting whilst I am at work.

The Girls subsiding into faint whispers, I dip my pen in the ink, and become suddenly conscious of the existence of partially smothered ferocity in the lower regions, accompanied by damage done to plates and dishes.

Really, this is not to be borne!

I throw down my pen, rush into the passage, and summon Dawkins.

"Dawkins," I say, "I want to speak to you."

"I want to speak to you, too," says Dawkins. "I should like to leave this house, if you have no objection."

Soothing Dawkins.

This is rather a staggerer, so I think it advisable to soothe Dawkins.

I say, "Dawkins, what have you to complain of?"

"What!" shrieks Dawkins, "what! Why, everything—particular that Tootsy!"

I think Dawkins requires more soothing on a different plan. I therefore invite her into my study, and impress upon her that although it is not advisable to let Tootsy hear what we think of her just yet awhile, I myself think very little of her indeed, and, what is more, do not intend to put up with her nonsense much longer. These sentiments would appear to afford some satisfaction to Dawkins, and she retreats to the lower regions with a significant wink.

A minute afterwards Tootsy taps at the door and
says, "You'll excuse me, sir, but this can't go on."

I say, "What can't, Mrs. Tootsy?"

She says, "That woman's owdaciousness."

Of course I know she means Dawkins, but as I am
not positive Dawkins is not listening at the moment,
I content myself with a mysterious nod.

Soothing Tootsy.

This, however, is not enough for Tootsy. She raises
her voice, and says she can't stand it, and, what is
more, she won't!

I assure her, in a whisper, that there is no occasion,
as it won't last long.

This is diplomatic. I don't tell her that it is she
who is likely to be the first to go.

But she won't have diplomacy. She says, "Either
that woman leaves, or I do."

To which I say, "Certainly."

To which she says, "Which is it to be, then?"

To which I say, "Why need you ask, my dear Mrs. Tootsy?"

To which she says, "I want a straightforward answer."

I am on the point of giving an answer, which is to be as straightforward as possible under the circumstances, when the door flies wide open, and Dawkins enters with clenched fists.

There will be some unpleasantness, I expect.

CHAPTER XI.

IN WHICH THE SOOTHING SYSTEM FAILS.

WHEN I said there would be unpleasantness, I was right.

There has been. Nay, there is still. I find myself at this moment occupying a position somewhat analogous to that of a railway buffer in a case of collision, and I have not only to meet the arguments adduced with calmness and composure, but at the same time to keep my legs.

The difficulty of so doing, as both Dawkins and Tootsy are what may be termed substantial women, with a tendency to bounce, is extreme, and I find myself in the middle of conciliatory observations with my boots in the air, and my body at angles not easily reconcilable with the proper maintenance of equilibrium. I also bump my head rather sharply against the wall.

The substance of the argument put forward, at the top of Dawkins's voice, is, that she sees this is no longer the house for her ; whilst the conclusion arrived at by Tootsy, at the top of *her* voice, is, that no power

Soothing everybody.

on earth would induce her to remain another moment beneath my roof. There are also casual allusions to the deceitfulness of double-faced deceivers, and to a pack of meddlesome Molly-coddles, which I pass over as unworthy of serious consideration.

By this time the Girls have gathered around, and Bathsheba exclaims, "Brother! how dare those women talk to you like that ?"

This is an unfortunate remark on the part of Bathsheba, as Tootsy and Dawkins immediately turn round upon her and indignantly demand whom she means by women.

Cassandra here says, "How dare you talk to your master in such a way? You ought to be ashamed of yourselves!"

This is also rather an unfortunate remark on the part of Cassandra, as it is immediately met with an observation to the effect that the master in question would be all the better for a lot more talking to, and a precious good shaking as well.

On this, Ursula, carried away by very natural indignation, says, "Brother, turn them both out of the house this very moment!"

Probably, on the whole, this is the most unfortunate remark of all three.

*　　*　　*　　*　　*　　*

Dawkins and Tootsy are no longer beneath my roof. It is not absolutely necessary to go into details. There may, or may not, have been a certain amount of unseemliness, accompanied by loss of dignity. In such cases there usually is.

One thing is certain, they are both gone. Gone, never to return.

After the excitement of the events that have just transpired, naturally succeeds a period of comparative reaction, in which the idea occurs to somebody that a new nurse will have to be found for those twins, and that (they are both on full pipe at this moment) pretty sharply.

Another idea occurs to somebody else immediately afterwards that it was rather awkward Dawkins should have left to-day, as we expect company to dinner.

On this I say, "We must all put our shoulders to the wheel."

"What!" says Bathsheba, "before we roast it?"

The company has come. The company is Pincher —Captain Pincher, my old companion in arms—and a man whom any other man might be proud to know.

I have no hesitation in saying that I am proud to

Pincher.

know Pincher, and I look upon it as an honour to my mahogany for Pincher to put his legs under it. I have frequently said as much to the Girls.

As to what the Girls have said in reply, that is immaterial. In questions of suitability as regards men, I have observed that the judgment of girls is not reliable. Therefore—though I have reason to believe that the Girls do not value Pincher's society as much as they should do—I am thoroughly determined that there shall be no more misalliances in our family, and that if any one of the Girls wants to get married, now is the time and here is the man!

We are at table. The meal has been prepared. We have prepared it. I myself have read the directions for roasting veal from the cookery book, and the Girls have acted under my instructions. I feel proud of the way in which this veal has been roasted, and my pride culminates in the happy blending of the ingredients with which it has been stuffed, and which, even tasted raw, though suety in parts, is, on the whole, a combination of unusual merit.

It is extraordinary how careless an ordinary cook is in the matter of ingredients. A search of the hitherto sacred precincts ruled over by Dawkins has resulted in the discovery that we are out of almost everything requisite for veal stuffing; and, mark my words, if Dawkins had still been here, the stuffing would have been made without them. As it is, they are not omitted. They have been fetched—some of them a considerable distance. We are all of us rather knocked up by the time the roast veal is ready, but we are proud of what we have done.

Pincher is here, as, I think, I have already observed, and I get him artfully on to the subject of his favourite joints, and next throw in roast veal in a loose and careless kind of way. On which Pincher, apparently not seeing my drift, says candidly he prefers any other joint. This is awkward; and there is no time to cook anything else.

I therefore break it to Pincher, that when he sees the veal he sees his dinner; at which he says, with some confusion, that when he said he did not care for roast veal, he meant because it was generally served up underdone.

On this I smile a smile of triumph, and cut a slice.
......It *is* rather pinkish inside, but that will do for the
Girls and me.

By the way, it is rather odd, but I never before observed a tendency on the part of Pincher to tell tedious
tales. He has been at it all dinner-time, and he is at
it now. In consequence of an accident to the jam
roley-poley, one of the Girls is detained a good while
downstairs, and another Girl goes after her to see what
is the matter, and then, as neither return, the third
Girl goes ; and then Pincher, who has in turn fixed
each with his eye as he has gone on with one of his
confoundedly long-winded narratives, wheels sharply
round and fixes me, and goes on still.

And at this moment I hear the twins upstairs begin
to howl with all their might and main.

I can't stand this. I cut Pincher short, and go to
see to the twins myself.

The Major : his agony.

CHAPTER XII.

IN WHICH THE MAJOR MAKES THE ACQUAINTANCE OF SOME CHARMING GIRLS.

IT is extraordinary how many times I have been compelled to point out to the Girls—kindly yet firmly —that I, Major Penny, might as well be consulted upon questions of moment relating to the domestic economy of the home circle.

It is extraordinary how often I have had to mention this fact, and it is even more extraordinary what a little notice has been taken of the fact when mentioned.

Take the case of Tootsy. Was I, or was I not, consulted relative to the engagement of Tootsy? No. Has that engagement, or has not that engagement, proved a failure? and have not unseemly brawls resulted therefrom?

Certainly.

Very well, then.

"Very well, then, Major," (I am usually thus addressed by the Girls), "why don't you go and try and find a new nurse yourself, and see how you like it?"

As may have been noticed, I am a man of few words, and on this occasion I use none. I rise from the breakfast-table, on the contrary, with a quiet smile, and go in search of my shoes in the passage.

As we are quite out of servants just now, I find that my shoes want cleaning, but I am too proud-spirited to mention it; so I do what I can in the privacy of my study with the lower part of one of the window-curtains, and put the shoes on afterwards with the aid of a paper-knife and pocket-handkerchief, in consequence of the shoe-horn not being forthcoming, and my being still too proud-spirited to ask whether anybody has seen it.

Having put my shoes on, I put on my hat and gloves, and, with the same quiet smile, descend the steps, cross the garden, and go forth on to the high road.

I feel certain that the Girls are dying to know where I am going to, and are peeping at me from places of concealment; but I take no notice of them, and pursue my way.

The corner of the road turned, it occurs to me that I am not quite certain which way mine is, and what I mean to do.   But this is not a moment for hesitation. I have, as it were, tacitly pledged myself to find a new nurse, and a new nurse I must find, or my position as head of our family circle is in jeopardy.   Also, that nurse must be an improvement on Tootsy, or I am nowhere.

As may possibly have been gleaned from remarks already made, there is a certain straggliness about our neighbourhood that necessitates a considerable amount of pedestrian exercise if one would commune with one's kind.

There are long straight roads going up the sides of steep hills, and other long straight roads on the other side going down the hills, with about one house on either side.

There is the parish church all by itself, with the

parson's house and the clerk's cottage quite half a mile away from it, but yet so much nearer to it than anybody else's house, it is not to be wondered at much if the two officials have occasionally had the church all to themselves when the weather has been bad.

Added to the isolation of our dwelling-places is a strict exclusiveness, which causes nobody to be on visiting terms with any one else, and courtships among

Rosabel's Sisters.

neighbouring gentility are never heard of. The Girls have noticed this particularly.

Among the native lower orders there is, of course, some difference. They do not, as well as I can understand, marry with precipitation, but they have enormous families when married. Why should not a member of one of these families take charge of the twins?

In the distance I observe a cottage which I know to

be densely populated, and I approach and inquire.
No ; there 's nursing enough to be done at home without going to look for it. I try another tightly-packed
cottage with the same result, and walk away into space
up a deuce of a hill.

I am awfully tired, but am too proud-spirited to
give in. A third cottage meets my view, or rather, a
small villa residence, semi-detached, and I determine

"Yes, ma !"

to ask an amiable middle-aged lady sitting in the front
garden whether she knows of any unemployed nurse
in the neighbourhood.

The middle-aged lady is as amiable as she looks.
She says, "Bless me ! where are my girls, I wonder?"
Then calls "Beatrix ! Maud ! Aurora !"

To this, three musical young voices respond, "Yes,
ma ! What is it ? "

"My loves," says the elderly lady, "come here, I beg of you."

And then there is a gentle rustle of skirts and a pattering of brass-tipped heels, and three graceful young creatures appear upon the steps, and listen to the elderly lady's version of my request.

Rosabel.

"Oh, ma!" exclaims one of them, "it is the very thing for Rosabel."

And then all three cry "Rosabel!" in chorus, and Rosabel, who is, to my thinking, the nicest of the four, comes tripping out, and entwines herself with her sisters, who are already entwined beneath the honey-suckle over the doorway.

"And is this Rosabel?" I murmur, as I beckon to her to approach and pat her on the head, "and would she be equal to twins?"

"Oh, yes, I am sure she would," cry Beatrix, Maud,

and Aurora, in musical chorus; "wouldn't you, Rosa-bel, dearest?"

This is very nice. This is really very nice indeed! I wonder what the Girls at home will say now?

"And the other—young ladies," I say with hesitation (I can hardly speak of them otherwise than as young ladies), "what do they do?"

"Beatrix wishes to go out as parlourmaid," says the elderly lady, "Maud as housemaid, and Aurora as cook."

If I were to engage all of them!

Stop a bit, though! What will the Girls at home say if I do?

CHAPTER XIII.

IN WHICH THE MAJOR HAS DOUBTS.

IN a general way, I am not in the habit of consulting the Girls, except, perhaps, at meal-times, when asking them whether they will take another help.

Hitherto, as Comptroller of our Home Circle, I have reason to believe I. have performed the duties devolving on me to the satisfaction of all concerned, with, possibly, the exception of the Butcher and Baker, the Grocers, Green and Family, the Milkman and the Washerwoman, whose accounts, I am proud to say, I am in the habit of auditing with a scrupulous attention to details.

Upon those occasions when I have thought it necessary to make any alteration in our domestic arrangements—for instance, to buy new carpets, or have the ceilings whitewashed—I have found it as well to mention, casually, what was my intention, but that was all. In the case of Tootsy, my directions had simply been, "Find a suitable person;" and it was, perhaps, unreasonable on my part, as we were pressed for time, to expect the Girls to trot out samples of the Tootsy tribe for me to select from, the more so as probably the one sample they got was the only one getable.

Very well, then! In this instance it is I who have gone forth in search of a nurse, and my success has been triumphant.

I have got a nurse, and more than that, I have got a cook. Not the ordinary nurse and cook usually found in the dwellings of the respectable middle classes, but two born ladies, willing to engage themselves in my service as Lady Helps!

Could anything more satisfactory possibly have happened? And yet it is a most extraordinary thing —I have some doubts whether the Girls at home will altogether approve of Rosabel and Aurora.

We are, by the way, not to call them by those sweet names—at least, not yet awhile—until we are on a more friendly footing. Their name is Montgomery, and when we want anything, we must either put it somehow this way, "I beg your pardon, Miss Aurora Montgomery, but, labouring under the impression that you have inadvertently overlooked the replenishment of the mustard-pot, I should deem it a favour were you to mix a little in an egg-cup, and bring it up as soon as convenient,"—or go down and mix the mustard yourself.

The question is, will the Girls fall into this new style, which, it must be allowed, when compared to talks with the late Dawkins, necessitates the employment of a syllable or two extra?

Yet, why should they object? Confound it all! I really cannot see why on earth they should object; and, what's more——

There they all are at the door.

Ahem!

You may have noticed, perhaps, that, as a rule, you feel more resolute when you press your hat down firmly, and keep your elbows close into your sides, at the same time straightening your knees and throwing the greater part of your weight on to the heel. It is also a good plan to hum a martial air, if one comes handy.

There is deep solicitude depicted on the visages of the Girls, and they say "Well?" in chorus as I approach.

I am not exactly clear why I say so, but I *do* say, "Well, what?"

"About the nurse," cry the Girls, still in chorus.

"Oh," I respond carelessly, as I hang my hat up, "that's all right, and—a new cook, too."

Now I come to think of it, is it all right, though? It really was a maid-of-all-work we wanted, not a cook only. Certainly, there are Beatrix and Maud, who desire places as housemaid and parlourmaid, but should I be justified in increasing our establishment at this rate, and what would the Girls——

I can't understand the Girls. They seem so awfully delighted I have been successful.

"A nice quiet motherly person, this nurse is, I am sure?" says Cassandra.

"One who has had a large family of her own, and thoroughly understands what's wanted by a family—when young?" says Bathsheba.

Good gracious! If Rosabel only heard that!

"And the cook," cries Ursula, "she is sober, of course?"

Rather more good graciouser! If Aurora did happen to be listening at the keyhole!

This is an evening in which strategy has to be mingled with what I might almost feel inclined to denominate confounded whackers; and when, after I have read prayers, the hour of retiring to rest approaches, I take up my flat candlestick oppressed by the consciousness of a truth which will take a goodish bit of breaking presently.

    *   *   *   *   *   *

Next morning, returning from a constitutional, I find the Girls once more assembled on the door-step. This time, evidently, events of a surprising nature have occurred.

Ursula trips down to the garden gate and breaks it to me.

"Oh, Major, what a while you have been, and two ladies have been waiting for you in the drawing-room almost ever since you have been gone!"

This somehow comes rather suddenly on me, for I feel certain I know who the two ladies are. Certainly, before this, I ought to have been prepared with an explanation ; and so, indeed, I have been, only I forget it again just at this moment. However, here goes!

As I thought, Aurora and Rosabel! And now to introduce them to the Girls. Aurora and Rosabel have risen from their seats, graceful, dignified, calm. Bathsheba, Cassandra, and Ursula regard them with an expression which is not absolutely enthusiastic.

It is for me to speak.

Now for it!

————o————

CHAPTER XIV

IN WHICH THE YOUNG LADIES CARRY ALL BEFORE THEM.

I HAVE done it.

It is over.

When I get a little bit cooler, I will endeavour to call to mind the exact particulars, but at present I hardly feel equal to a mental effort on so large a scale.

Yet it is positively preposterous that I (Major Penny—I fancy I have mentioned my name once before) should find myself wanting in words—nay, absolutely almost tongue-tied — respecting trifles wholly unworthy of serious consideration. Nevertheless, I am not sorry it is all over, and that the Girls clearly understand that Rosabel and Aurora are our new nurse and cook. I confess I do not quite understand what the Girls' private sentiments are upon the subject, in

The Old Girls and the New Girls.

consequence of their having hitherto maintained a silence which can only be described as ice-bound.

I, on the other hand, having recovered myself a little, am, if possible, verging on the other extreme, and am excessively voluble.

I casually remark, "You will find, I fear, Miss Aurora Montgomery, that the culinary arrangements

Another addition.

in the lower story are wanting in completeness, as the last cook—I mean the person who officiated below—had a habit of burning the bottoms out of things. Cassandra, however, will show you everything. Or," I add, observing that in Cassandra's expression there is no indication of a probability of her doing anything of the kind, "I will."

　　*　　　*　　　*　　　*　　　*　　　*

It is very strange how the breeding of the True

Lady manifests itself in trifling details. Nothing could be more urbane than the deportment of the Misses Montgomery, and they even carry their high-bred dissimulation of unconsciousness with respect to what I might almost denominate as the defiant snortiness of the Girls to the extent that they seem to be patronizing the Girls, and the Girls don't seem to like it.

However, we shall see what we shall see !

* * * * * *

We have ! I never remember to have sat down to a more perfectly served dinner. It is true that the *pièce de résistance* happens to be the cold roast beef left over from yesterday, with *entrées* of mashed potatoes and mixed pickles, but it is the style in which the things are placed upon the table that I look at.

Bathsheba's mood is still unpropitious. She says, "I like my potatoes cooked with salt."

———o———

CHAPTER XV.

IN WHICH SOMETHING IS KNOCKED DOWN TO THE MAJOR.

'T IS occasionally a pleasant change to stroll at eventide up the high road. As a rule there is but little excitement ; but this evening there is a sale at the

6

Auctioneer's, and I drop in and look round. I have
no intention of buying anything. I have frequently
dropped in before with the same intention, or rather
want of intention, but I have found it to be an agree-
able way of wiling away a spare half-hour.

At the auction-room there is generally a gathering
of the neighbouring gentry, who drop in to look at the
effects of those among their neighbours who are being
sold up, and derive a kind of melancholy pleasure from

"Going!"

the contemplation of other people's household gods
going off dirt cheap.

The population of these parts not being numerous,
these sales do not occur often enough to grow common, and the excitement they offer is ever welcome.
This evening the room is more than usually well attended, and I enter and nod smilingly to the right and
to the left, and neighbours on the right and left nod
back at me.

The furniture being sold this evening belonged to a
purse-proud *parvenu*, who came and settled down here
the winter before last, and was extremely supercilious

in his tone towards the neighbouring gentry. Things, however, went wrong with the purse-proud *parvenu's* business in the City, and we have now the satisfaction of seeing him sold up. A Butcher and a Grocer whom he let in rather stiffly watch the prices things fetch with a certain amount of eagerness.

I am really glad I did not miss the sale this evening. I have reason to believe that my presence is looked forward to at any assembly of a public character in the neighbourhood; and though I am not quite sure

Another good Perambulator gone wrong.

that the Auctioneer is always quite as respectful as he ought to be, I observe with satisfaction that to-night he is smiling at me blandly.

I will nod to him.

I have.

* * * * * *

This is really a very interesting sale. The purse-proud *parvenu's* goods are, as everybody always

thought, of the most gimcrack character, and as each
lot falls under the hammer at some paltry price, everybody but the Butcher and Grocer smile pleasantly.
The Butcher and Grocer are beginning to have doubts
whether there will be much left for them when the
bill of sale is settled.

But time goes, and so must I. One of the Auctioneer's
men stops me.

He says, "Will you clear the perambulator to-night,
sir?"

Insubordination in the ranks.

I inquire in amazement, "What perambulator?"
"The one that was knocked down to you! Twelve
and six."

A light dawns on me. This comes of nodding to
the Auctioneer. Shall I indignantly repudiate the
perambulator? My first impulse is to do so; but then
everybody is looking at me, and I fancy I hear a dis-
tinct snigger.

Besides, now I come to think of it, the twins really

ought to have a perambulator. It is most unreasonable to expect that Miss Rosabel Montgomery can drag about two hulking boys of that kind without mechanical aid.

Besides, also, it is only twelve and sixpence, and I don't see how I can get out of paying with any dignity.

* * * * * *

I have paid now. The perambulator is mine, and I have chartered a boy to wheel it home for me.

Awkwardness.

The boy turns out to be a fool of a boy, with no command over his limbs. He wheels the perambulator in front of him, and somehow the wheel sticks fast, and he and the perambulator come to grief.

I am not aware whether the reader of this history ever fell over a perambulator, but, if not, it may be casually mentioned that it is a deuce of a thing to get clear away from when you once begin falling.

I have got this boy out of the tangle, and have slapped his head, and now he refuses to wheel the perambulator any more.

After all, the road is a lonely one, and very dark. Why should I not wheel it myself? Good gracious!

Two elegant young ladies approach.

I do not know them. Yes, I do! They are the other two Misses Montgomery — Miss Beatrix and Miss Maud. How confoundedly awkward!

CHAPTER XVI.

IN WHICH NOTHING COULD BE NICER THAN IT IS.

I AM not without certain secret misgivings with regard to the policy of going in heavily for Lady Helps. I should be inclined to advise, if you want my opinion upon the subject, that one is enough to try at a time where there are many unmarried girls in the house, particularly if the girls are of mature age.

I have no doubt that the experience of married men may prove happier, and I should imagine that a young Lady Help would be just what a middle-aged married lady would like to introduce into her establishment; but, in the case of a household where there are unmarried girls of a mature age, it is calculated to lead to unkindly feelings, and possibly even come to slaps.

At the same time it must be allowed that nothing could be more considerate than the behaviour of Rosabel and Aurora towards the Girls.

The truth is, the Girls have not been brought up to domestic duties. Bathsheba at an early age went in for old china, whilst Cassandra took to water-colours, and Ursula to the four-finger exercise. In each branch of study one or other of the Girls excels, and in Berlin woolwork, in all its branches, I am ready to maintain that the Girls have no equals.

There has, up to now, been no occasion for the Girls to perform duties of a menial character. I am not a man of large means, but I have a little independency which entitles me to cultivate the refinements of life; and I would prefer that my sisters—the Girls—should continue to collect china (in moderation), to paint views (of adjacent scenery) in water-colours, and to practise the four-finger exercise (within limits).

I must confess I am surprised the Girls have not entered with more enthusiasm into this practical test of the question of Lady Helps, which theoretically has, to my certain knowledge, met with much approval at my own dinner-table.

I trust I have made myself sufficiently understood to have avoided a possible misconstruction respecting the Girls' behaviour towards Rosabel and Aurora. The Girls have made no open resistance. They would not venture to do so when I have once expressed a wish; but there is a want of responsiveness which, I fear, must tend to make Rosabel and Aurora feel uncomfortable.

For my own part, I am doing all I can to cause a

contrary impression. My first step has been to see that the dormitory allotted to them is equal to the occasion. The Girls appear to think that the spare bed-room we set apart for an occasional guest is not, perhaps, the one that should be used, and Cassandra says, "Won't Dawkins's room do for them?"

I have a look at the room that did for Dawkins, and rather wonder it didn't do for her in another sense. Although there is a superabundance of roof to Dawkins's room, which comes in contact with your head when you turn round if not in the habit of ducking to avoid it, there is a hole in the roof through which the rain is just now dripping.

The window is, in itself, not a bad sort of window, if it were placed so that the light could get in through it, and it ought to shut an inch or two tighter.

I suppose Dawkins must have been rather tired of a night, or I don't see how she could have slept in that bed ; and I dare say she found it handier to lift her washstand jug without a handle, or she might possibly have mentioned it.

I suppose, too, lots of people don't care about having a soap-dish or a tooth-glass.

If the Misses Montgomery are to occupy the disgraceful cockloft vacated by Dawkins, we want the plumbers, glaziers, and painters here at once, and a cart-load of furniture to follow. Under these circumstances, I don't see how we can do better than allow the young Lady Helps to occupy the spare room for a night.

I have indicated their apartment to Miss Aurora, and she has gone into it with a graceful inclination.

Miss Rosabel is at this moment asking Bathsheba for
a few large-sized Baden bath towels, and has just sug-
gested that the position of the toilet-table shall be
changed to one more desirable as regards reflection.

*　　*　　*　　*　　*　　*

The morning meal is upon the table punctually to

Aurora on Hash.

the very moment we fixed upon overnight. I am
ashamed to say I myself am not quite ready for it. I
wonder whether the Girls are?

The Girls are not, thank goodness! and I am down
first, and just able to pour out a cup of coffee, butter a
bit of toast, and begin breaking the shell of an egg,
before the first one descends.

"Really, Bathsheba," I exclaim, "you must endeavour to be punctual. It gives no encouragement!"

Bathsheba's face wears an expression indicative of smouldering, as she silently helps herself to a piece of lukewarm bacon. Meanwhile I go on with my lukewarm egg, and don't think I care for an egg at that temperature when only slightly cooked.

If I saw my way clear, I think I should pocket this

Rosabel on Nursing.

egg surreptitiously, whilst Bathsheba was looking another way; but an underdone egg with a hole in it is such a messy thing to carry! Besides, there would be inquiries about the shell. Suppose I leave the egg uneaten? But I can't very well do that; it might hurt Aurora's feelings.

＊　　＊　　＊　　＊　　＊　　＊

I have been for a stroll across the hill, and had a sandwich at an inn on the other side, and am now on my way back to lunch.

As I open the street door I hear a Babel of female voices. Everybody seems to be talking at once ; but I have observed that this is the ordinary method of carrying on a conversation between women. Is it a

The Twins at it.

row? No. The Girls are actually pal-ing on (if I may use such a term) with Rosabel and Aurora.

At this moment but one voice is audible. It is Aurora's, and she is expatiating on the advantages accruing from the proper seasoning of minced beef, at which the Girls are expressing wonder and delight.

And now it is Rosabel, who is briefly running through the duties of a nurse, with the view to showing that a child need never cry if properly managed. How nice this is!——What's that?

The twins at this moment are howling their loudest upstairs. I mention the fact as I enter, and whilst Rosabel goes to look after them, Aurora places the hash upon the table.

    *   *   *   *   *   *

"Now," cries Ursula, ecstatically—"now, Major, you must taste this!"

I do.

I have.

It tastes smoky.

Tasting the hash.

CHAPTER, XVII.

IN WHICH A BOLD SOLDIER COMES MARAUDING.

THIS is very nice!

Of course I knew from the first that the Girls would not keep on acting unreasonably, but I was inclined to think that their unreasonableness would have lasted longer. It was, I thought, possible that the Misses Montgomery had been rather too much of a shock to the Girls. Since then things have shaken down, and general joy prevails.

This is very nice!

Hallo!

*   *   *   *   *   *

A remarkably bold-looking soldier has just passed by the house, tapping his chin with the end of his cane, and ogling my upper story.

A detachment of the Onety-oneth were expected to be quartered shortly in Hagglebury, our nearest market town. I did not know they had come down yet, but such is evidently the case. Bathsheba and Ursula have entered into the matter with something like enthusiasm. They say it will make Hagglebury quite gay, but Cassandra is inclined to think that the advent of redcoats may tend towards carryings on, more especially in the case of the Hagglebury servant-girls. On this, Bathsheba very properly points out that the Hagglebury servant-girls are staid and proper

servant-girls, and not at all like the servant-girls elsewhere, and that if the soldiers come there with an idea
of carrying on, they will find that they have come to
the wrong place.

Meanwhile what I want to know is, why that bold
soldier ogled my upper story? Surely to goodness
Bathsheba and Ursula would not encourage——

However, he is gone now, and I have an important
letter I wish to send off this morning to the editor of
the "Times," relative to a singularly simple, though
curiously ingenious, Colorado beetle-trap which has
just occurred to me; from which, when the Colorado
beetle has once got in, it will be absolutely impossible
to dislodge him without breaking the trap. It is most
extraordinary that this idea has never occurred to
anybody before, and certainly I must lose no time in
putting it down on paper.

    *   *   *   *   *   *

I have been much longer putting it down than I
expected to be. Though the trap when made would
be simplicity itself, I find that it has taken upwards
of seven hundred words to explain it with anything
approaching to lucidity; and even now I am not quite
sure that I could understand it if it had been written
by some one else, and were read to me for the first time.

Perhaps it will be best to defer sending to the
"Times" to-day, and to take a walk over the hill and
back just to clear my head, and then read the thing
through quietly.

I am half-way up the hill when I observe an object
upon its brow, standing out against the sky as though
it were on the extreme limit of the earth in that

direction, and must either topple over or turn back. It turns back, however, and, as it approaches nearer, I discover it to be the same bold military man again.

But why the deuce is he coming this way? His way to Hagglebury is over the hill in the opposite direction. Has he lost it?

It may be unnecessary to point out to the reader, who has the advantage of Mr. Chasemore's somewhat flippant, though on the whole trustworthy, sketches to refer to, that my aspect when in repose is martial. I have recently, however, suffered somewhat severely from my feet, and have not that firmness of tread which accompanied my movements on the tented field. As the distance between this same bold soldier and me gradually lessens, I pull myself together as much as possible, and, holding my head erect, step forth.

I may be wrong, but I am under the impression that when this soldier's eye meets mine he will salute me. I shall then enter into conversation with him and ascertain particulars.

    *   *   *   *   *   *

I *was* wrong; but it has been the result of unforeseen circumstances. I met his eye, but he did not salute me. At the moment I met it I kicked a loose stone with my big toe, and made a face. The bold soldier was pleased to grin at this accident or the face I made, and he has passed on without any conversation being entered into.

At this moment I hardly feel inclined for conversation. I am standing on one leg, nursing the injured toe in my hand, and I dare say I am making a series of faces.

Looking after the bold soldier, I meet his eye as he turns his head. He is still grinning.

*   *   *   *   *   *

My toe is better now. I have been over the hill, and am upon my way home again.

I have cleared my head, and intend to go thoroughly into the Colorado beetle-trap. It occurs to me that if the total destruction of the traps is an absolute necessity in every case of emptying, the expense of continually getting new traps may be urged as a drawback. I must endeavour to meet this objection, however, without loss of time.

Hallo!

*   *   *   *   *   *

Accidentally looking through the parlour window on my way to my study, I observe the selfsame bold soldier, with his legs much straddled, standing directly in front of my house, and again ogling my upper story.

"Confound you, fellow! How dare you?"

He has not heard me, because the window is shut. But he ought to see me shaking my fist. Somehow, however, he doesn't; and now he has gone on again, and——. No; it can't be—yes, it is, though—*kissing his hand!*

Upon my soul, this is really too bad of Bathsheba and Ursula!

I cannot for a moment conceive that they have done anything to warrant such a liberty on the part of the said bold soldier; but what I complain of is their imprudence in showing themselves at the windows at all; for I am aware, from experience, that the very smallest amount of encouragement is necessary.

The bold Soldier : his carryings on.

"Bathsheba! Ursula! are you upstairs?"

They are, and they descend in answer to my summons. I fix them with my eye. There is decidedly an unusual colour upon the faces of both, and most undoubtedly they quail beneath my glance.

Bathsheba, with an unwonted sprightliness, says, "Major, the Onety-oneth have arrived. There have been several pass by this morning."

This is nice news! Have the others kissed their hands too, I wonder? We shall have all the regiment down here at it to-morrow. Stay, though: is it possible the Girls have been carried away by the novelty of the occurrence, and have not recognized this fellow to be the same soldier passing and repassing?

"What very fine men they are!" exclaims Ursula.

Upon second thoughts, I will not at present say what I intended to say to the Girls, but will watch the course of events.

Lunch is ready now. How punctual Miss Aurora is! Irish stew, and yet how unlike any Irish stew I have ever tasted before! In fact, quite a pleasant change, with something of the flavour of *à la mode* beef! Henceforth our *cuisine* will not be wanting in variety.

*   *   *   *   *   *

There was something in that stew beyond the ordinary filling properties of stew, and I really now feel quite disinclined to go into the beetle-trap. I will, therefore, go for a walk instead.

I go across the fields at the back of my house, and compose my thoughts on my favourite stile till I feel rather sleepy, and then return. As I approach my garden wall, the sound of a musical voice falls upon my ear. It belongs to Miss Rosabel. She is reciting the poem of "Baby Bunting." Hitherto I have failed to see much poetry in B. B.; but now, how different!

If I thought she would not observe me, I should really very much like to take a peep over the wall. I will.

"Now, then, old What's-o'clock, none o' that!"

It is the bold soldier tugging at my coat-tails.

"Leave go, fellow!"

"Not me. You leave the young gal alone, will you? You ought to be ashamed of yourself!"

CHAPTER XVIII.

IN WHICH A SELECT COMPANY ARE ENTERTAINED WITH TEA AND A LITTLE MUSIC.

THE bold soldier has gone about his business, and we are going on most satisfactorily.

I have not deemed it necessary to refer to the bold soldier in the presence of Miss Rosabel, or before the Girls.

A certain amount of disrespect manifested by the bold soldier may possibly be reported at the proper quarters, but, at present, the matter is under my consideration, and me alone it concerns.

The bold soldier, at any rate, has temporarily departed, and, unless he comes again, I am inclined to allow bygones to be bygones.

Meanwhile, I narrowly watch the conduct of the Misses Montgomery and the Girls, and I see nothing in the former to lead me to suppose that they, at any time, were conscious of the bold soldier's existence. In the latter, however, there is possibly less steadfastness of purpose, and I observe that the Girls look out of window a good deal, though, at present, I am unable to decide whether they always did do so, or that the habit has been but recently acquired.

     *   *   *   *   *   *

In other respects, nothing could well be more satisfactory than the way we are getting on—on the new system.

We are now unanimously agreed that we never will return to the irksome bondage of the past. In the dark days of Dawkins, when Dawkins cooked for us, and washed and brushed up for us, it was positively dangerous to approach Dawkins with even a suggestion, and it must have been a bold individual indeed who would have ventured to lay a hand on Dawkins's housework. How different now!

In the morning the Girls assist Miss Aurora in preparing the breakfast, washing up the breakfast-things, and making the beds, and there is not one unkind word—one cross look.

Again, in the nursery, over and over again, one Girl will take one twin, and another the other, and bath and bottle him, whilst Miss Rosabel looks on with a pleasant smile.

In the dark days of Dawkins it was as much as your life was worth to ask for your shaving-water before Dawkins brought it, should you, in consequence of your watch being wrong, fancy Dawkins had forgotten it. Now you can go out upon the landing and call half a dozen times for it without giving offence.

The Major's consideration.

Again, would Dawkins ever have allowed you to carry your own coals upstairs? No. Whereas now I invariably do so, without the slightest approach to discussion upon the subject.

It may be here mentioned that this experiment of ours, of the employment of Lady Helps, has created a profound sensation among the neighbouring gentry, and, with the exception of Lady Taltorkington (who still labours under the impression that I am deranged), we have had visits from all the best families, and have been literally overwhelmed with inquiries.

If everything continues satisfactorily, it is possible that the ordinary servant-girl will entirely vanish from the domestic circles in these parts; and I have already begun to prepare a letter to the editor of the "Times," which, when it appears, will, I have reason to believe, cause a profound sensation.

More consideration on the part of the Major.

*   *   *   *   *   *

An idea has just occurred to Cassandra, and she trips into my study to communicate it.

"Major," she says, "I have just made a most delightful discovery. Dear Aurora is an accomplished musician. This evening the Robinson girls are coming, and Mr. Jackson and Mr. Johnson. Supposing, after tea, we have dear Aurora up to play to them?"

The idea appears to me to be an admirable one, and I readily acquiesce. The Robinson girls are well-meaning, and act according to their lights; but their range of vision is limited and their experience small. They are, in fact, just exactly the kind of persons who would naturally be prejudiced against anything partaking of the nature of innovation, particularly when on a scale of such magnitude as the employment of the highly educated on the maid-of-all-work system. I shall look forward to this evening, and anticipate triumphant results.

    *   *   *   *   *   *

The company having arrived, Rosabel, during a temporary lull among the twins, has opened the street door. The Robinson girls sail past her without taking any notice, but I observe that young Jackson, who accompanies them, opens his eyes very widely.

Old Johnson comes alone shortly afterwards, and is a long while hanging up his hat and overcoat.

Aurora brings up the tea.

Hitherto we have made no remark. We have allowed the company to gaze, but have maintained silence. When, however, the tea-things are removed, I state the case, and I have reason to believe that the company are rather surprised.

The eldest Miss Robinson says, "Don't you find it rather awkward to decide how to treat this class of persons?"

"Not in the least," I respond; "we treat them as though they were our own family."

"Oh!" says the eldest Miss Robinson.

I fancied that would surprise her; and I continue with a quiet smile, "You may have observed the faultless way in which the tea was made and handed round. We will, with your permission, allow sufficient time to elapse for the tea-things to be washed up, and then summon Miss Aurora—our cook and housemaid —to oblige us with a selection from the beauties of Beethoven on the pianoforte."

" Bless me ! " says old Johnson.

.＊　　＊　　＊　　＊　　＊　　＊

The time has come. The tea-things are washed up. We have had some of the beauties of Beethoven and other distinguished composers. We are now having a soprano song from the latest opera. Old Johnson is listening entranced, and young Jackson is hanging all over the piano.

The Robinson girls don't seem very rapturous. Prejudice again.

The other Girls are looking a little solemn.

Aurora shows signs of leaving off.

" Go on ; oh, pray go on ! " says young Jackson.

The pleasant Evening.

CHAPTER XIX.

IN WHICH THERE IS SOMETHING WRONG AGAIN.

IT must be confessed that I have my misgivings with regard to the experiment.

Undoubtedly the transfer of our young Lady Helps from the kitchen and nursery to the drawing-room has been, as far as old Johnson and young Jackson are concerned, an enormous success. I never knew old Johnson so lively. And as to young Jackson, it requires positive brute force to get him away from the piano to hand round the pound-cake and negus.

Where my misgiving comes in is with respect to the Robinson girls. Perhaps they really do not care for music. They somehow do not seem to be enjoying themselves.

With regard to Bathsheba, Cassandra, and Ursula, I do not exactly know what to think. It was certainly Cassandra's own suggestion that we should have in "dear Aurora" to play to us; but I cannot help fancying now that there is an expression on her face indicative of mixed feelings, inclusive of a desire to slap or pinch "dear Aurora" hard.

Undoubtedly there is reason to believe that the experiment has not been wholly successful, but, thank goodness! the evening is at an end.

For some time past the company have been divided, as it were, and estranged.

At one end of the room have sat silently the three

Penny Girls and the Girls Robinson, and a deathlike silence has prevailed amongst them. At the other end of the room Aurora and Rosabel are playing a duet, and old Johnson and young Jackson are crawling around, so to speak, with a cloyed look on them, like flies in summer-time amongst the moist sugar in a grocer's window. The centre of the apartment, a kind of neutral ground, is occupied by myself, Major Penny, who for a certain length of time regard the proceedings with a benignant smile, and then less benignantly.

At the end of the duet, wild applause from young Jackson on the lid of the piano (Cassandra's piano on the hire system, and I can see she doesn't like it). Also chuckle-headedness, and "brayvo! brayvo! brayvissimo!" from old Johnson, whilst deathlike silence still prevails among the Girls.

Then Aurora and Rosabel begin another duet, and then suddenly the eldest Girl Robinson rises, and says, with emphasis, to the Penny Girls, "I am afraid it is growing very late. The time *does* pass so rapidly when one is *amusing* oneself; and I am sure *these gentlemen* are! Ann, Jane" (to the other Girls Robinson), "we had better put on our bonnets. *Do, pray, come!*"

*   *   *   *   *   *

They have put on their bonnets. They have thanked us, with more emphasis, for a *very* pleasant evening, and they are gone.

So is that doddling old dotard of a Johnson. So is that empty-headed ass, young Jackson. Aurora and Rosabel have retired to their respective spheres;

Cassandra is trying the notes of her piano on the hire system to ascertain which are broken; Bathsheba says she has a headache; and Ursula has gone to bed.

I am not quite sure whether we ought to have many more of these kind of evenings.

But if we do, we won't have old Johnson and young Jackson again. No, thank you!

     *   *   *   *   *   *

And now to consider the experiment of an attractive young Lady Help from another point of view— with regard to the effect she is likely to have upon the local tradesmen's assistants, and the rank and file of the English army when quartered in the neighbourhood.

It has taken me some little time to thoroughly realize the fact; but, now it is realized, here it is. The soul of the young man from the Baker's is filled with ecstacy at the sight of Aurora. The young man from the Butcher's is a prey to conflicting emotions, amongst which are the deepest passion and the deadliest jealousy. If anything occurs to thwart that young man's aspirations (and I don't believe he has a chance), that young man wouldn't be safe to come near with a sticking-knife in his possession.

But perhaps the worst case of all is that of the young man from the Grocer's shop. I don't like to meet the eye of that young man. It is hollow, and has a hungry look in it. I should think, since Aurora began taking in our groceries, his services to his employer have been comparatively valueless.

A third of that young man's day appears to be taken up in leaving wrong packages at our house, and coming again to fetch them, or to ask whether he has accidentally left other packages of an apocryphal character.

So far Aurora downstairs.   Now as to Rosabel upstairs.

At this moment three bold soldiers are seated in front of some railings opposite my house, and are fixing and focussing Rosabel at the nursery window in a way which, taking the fact that I am shaking my fist at them like anything from the parlour window, is really perfectly incredible. How—I repeat the question—how dare they ?

*   *   *   *   *   *

It takes my breath away.

CHAPTER XX.

IN WHICH THE MAJOR THINKS THE TWINS OUGHT TO BE CALLED SOMETHING.

IT has just occurred to me (I trust I may be allowed to refer to the occurrence *en passant*) that the title of this work being the Twopenny Twins, there ought to be a little bit more about the twins in this work.

There shall be more.

It must not, however, be supposed that though I have lately been somewhat silent regarding the twins,

Extraordinary effects of the Aurora-Rosabel experiment.

that the twins themselves maintain the same reticence. If they could be squallier then they have been, they are.

I take it that the voice of innocent babyhood at its higher notes is a thing one may get to like in course of time, but I should say it took a long while.

*   *   *   *   *   *

The time has now arrived when the twins should have names to go by. Hitherto a numeral has suf-

Consulting the Dictionary.

ficed, but I am of opinion that it would be more desirable to call them something, and the question that naturally arises is, What?

In matters of this kind I have found that a consultation with the Girls is apt to lead to discussion. At any rate, it will be best to make my own mind up first, and the only question is, How?

Ah! an idea strikes me. What is this? "Nugent's New Pocket Dictionary of the French and English

Languages." I remember there is a list of names somewhere at the end. Here it is :—

, "Proper Names, Surnames, etc., etc., which Begin by a Different Letter in French."

No. 1 Name.— Abdias, Obadiah. How about Obadiah? That might save trouble, by the bye. The twins might be called the Two Obadiahs. Perhaps that wouldn't do, though, either. They would sound too much like a comic song.

Let me see again. Adelstan, Ethelstan. Ethelstan Twopenny sounds rather well.

Aggée, Haggée, Haggai. I don't care for those.

Alexandrette, Scanderoon. This is getting beyond me.

Allemagne, Germany. Angleterre, England. Oh, bother this!

Hallo! here's another list.

"Abbreviations of English and French Christian Names used in Familiar Discourse." Let's be familiar.

Assy, for Alice. That's rough on Alice's mental qualifications, it seems to me. Bat for Bartholomew. A Towpenny Bat wouldn't do. And what should the other be called? Ball, perhaps, or Stumps.

Bob for Robert, Dicky for Richard, Grit for Griffith, Jos for Joshua, Nobs for Obadiah. It's no good looking at this; it only distracts me. Let me think. There must be two names, of course, and there should be some connection between the two—such as Romulus and Remus. How about Romulus and Remus, by the bye? Stay, though, that wouldn't do! People would compare me to the wild beast that nursed them. Suppose I take a walk.

I have been walking some time, and nothing has yet occurred to me. Here is our Grocer's shop, with his name painted over it. His name is Jill. It suggests Jack and Jill. I always thought Jill was a girl's name. However, I won't call the twins Jack and Jill, and I have higher aims for them than fetching pails of water.

Bless me! who is that I see in the coffee-room of

Consulting Bagshaw.

the "White Lion"? My old friend Bagshaw, as I am alive—Bagshaw of ours! The very man to consult! A man who is always prompt and ready for action.

"How do, Bagshaw? How do, Captain? Glad to meet you."

Bagshaw doesn't seem so very glad, but that's his way. He is not a demonstrative man. He says he is well, and also mentions that since I met him last he has been promoted. Hang it all! I wish I had known that; but I couldn't see his uniform through the window. However, I congratulate him warmly when I get inside the room, and then break it to him about the twins.

"I want your advice, old fellow," I say. "I want a name for a boy baby."

He stares hard for half a minute, and then says "Wellington," with decision, and evidently thinks the matter settled.

Wellington Twopenny! I fancy that sounds rather well; but then there's the other twin. I put this to him hastily, as he is striding from the room. I say, "But I want two names." He turns on his heels, and faces me.

"What do you want two for?"

I say, "It's usual in a case of twins. What do you say to Napoleon for the other?"

"Confounded tomfoolery, sir!" he says, and goes off in a rage. Bagshaw was always rather an ass, it seems to me, and so confoundedly touchy!

I put on my hat again, and go farther.

Here's our curate Mr. Smale's house. I'll just drop in and put it to him. I tell him I have twins to provide for, and am short of names. He says it is a serious matter. I break Romulus and Remus to him, and he rejects them instantly as Pagan. Perhaps something Scriptural would meet with his approval. There is Ham and Shem; but I fancy there ought to be a Japheth, properly. I don't like to suggest Cain and Abel, but I venture on David and Goliath, and

he springs from his chair and asks me if I mean to
insult him.

Probably Goliath is not quite the right thing, and I
explain that it was a slip of the tongue. But Smale
gets quite warm about it, and won't be appeased. So
I give him a bit of my mind, and take my departure.

Insulting the Clergy.

Bless me!—why did I not think of it before?—there
is Lady Taltorkington, the person of all others to be
consulted. I will call on her this afternoon.

*   *   *   *   *   *

It seems to me she has not, as yet, quite got over
the impression that I am a lunatic. She fixes me
pretty steadily with her eye whilst I get through my
preliminary sentence. When I have got through it,
and say blandly, "Now, my dear Lady Taltorkington,
if you had twins, what would you call them?" she
starts indignantly to her feet, and rings the bell for
the servant to show me out.

*   *   *   *   *   *

The servant has done so. I have quitted Taltorkington Towers.

On reflection, it occurs to me that as Lady Taltorkington is a spinster who is notorious for her aversion to children, I was wrong in consulting her, and, possibly, I put the question rather the wrong way.

After all, it seems to me it is not I who, properly speaking, should have the responsibility of finding names for the twins. Oughtn't their Godfathers and Godmothers to do it?

Certainly.

Insulting the Gentry.

CHAPTER XXI.

IN WHICH THERE IS VERY NEARLY A TRAGEDY.

UNLESS I am labouring under a most extraordinary misapprehension, it distinctly states in your Catechism that your name is given to you by your Godfather and Godmother.

The question which naturally arises is, Whom shall I select for the office ?

This wants thinking over.

Let me think.

Stop a bit, though ; thought is at this moment out of the question—that is to say, thought on this subject.

The subject occupying the undivided attention of my household at this moment is Aurora's toothache.

When everything seemed going on—or, perhaps, I might say, on the point of going on—satisfactorily, Aurora's tooth began to ache.

It would be unreasonable and unfair to expect culinary feats from Aurora under these circumstances, and we neither expect them nor get them. At this moment Aurora is reclining, with her head tied up, upon the drawing-room sofa, and two of the Girls are endeavouring to soothe her sufferings, and persuade her to try infallible remedies, whilst the third Girl is making a kind of a stew, which we are to make a sort of meal of presently, when we have time.

Unfortunately the infallibles are on this occasion unavailing. They won't cure Aurora, who still reclines, and her head is still tied up.

The Girls implore me to seek medical aid. Aurora's blue orbs, fixed upon me, are full of plaintive entreaty. I hastily swallow a mouthful of the dish and crumble up a bit of bread, and seize my hat.

It would be selfish to think of food at such a moment, though I must confess that I am desperately hungry.

As I seize my hat, therefore, I seize a chunk of bread off the bread-plate in the hall, and a moment afterwards am choking on the high road without.

When I say medical aid, I own that this is putting the kind of aid one usually gets from one of our local doctors in rather a flattering light. We have two local doctors, and one of them is pretty good when sober, whilst the other is rather bad, generally. The pretty-good-when-sober local doctor is away from home— probably getting unsober—so I am obliged to go to the other doctor, and put it to him about the tooth.

He says, " Why don't she have it out ? "

I explain that she objects.

He says, " Bah ! "

I explain that Aurora is not quite sure which tooth it is that is aching, as all the jaw aches. On which he grunts, but offers no remark.

I say, finding a longish pause here, " Is there any kind of remedy you can suggest ? "

He makes no reply, but, rising to his feet (he has been seated hitherto), walks round the shop and reads the names on the bottles. As he does so, I follow his movements with my eye, and pass the time wondering whether he knows himself the meaning of the names, and why peppermint lozenges should be called what the bottle calls them.

After a time he appears to light unexpectedly upon a small quantity of white powder, which he weighs with elaboration, upsetting about half of it on the counter and the floor.

I ask what it is; but, as he is not in the habit of answering questions, he takes no notice, and I wait as patiently as I can.

Eventually, the packet being made, he looks for a pen in a couple of drawers, and, finding it at last under the counter, writes the word "Quinine" on it, and asks me for a shilling.

I return to find Aurora still reclining, and the Girls in great distress. The quinine is administered, and we await the results. They are almost immediate: Aurora is very sick.

I am much distressed. So are the Girls. Rosabel suggests that she should go home to their dear mamma, and fetch another infallible remedy mamma keeps always at hand ready prepared.

Aurora, however, elects to go herself. She thinks the change may do her good. We think so too.

*   *   *   *   *   *

Aurora has gone.

An interval of comparative calm is now ensuing. I have had some more of the dish. It doesn't taste very well cold; but never mind.

I am preparing a letter to the editor of the "Times," which occupies me longer than I expected, and one of

Aurora's Mamma.

the Girls taps at the door, and asks me whether I know what time it is. I look up at the clock.

Bless me! I had no idea it was so late.

"Oh! Major," says Cassandra, "we are in such a dreadful state about poor dear Aurora! She promised she would return directly, and it is three hours since she went out."

I suggest that perhaps her mamma has detained her; but I, too, am certainly rather uneasy.

Another hour has passed, yet Aurora has not returned. I seek my apartment, and wile away a little time in experiments with a patent hair-wash, which I believe I neglected to mention having purchased at the chemist's with the quinine. Whilst thus occupied, another of the Girls comes tapping.

"Oh, Major, we are so horribly frightened! Do you really think that was quinine you bought?"

"Do I what?" This is worse than Tootsy's Epsom salts! But stay. Do not let us be precipitate. One false alarm of that kind is surely enough. I know the taste of quinine perfectly, and here is the paper with a little yet in it. In my excitement I forget the dye upon my fingers.

Merciful goodness! It is not the least bit like quinine. What is to be done? I stagger towards the street door, and my knees knock together as I go. But suddenly the street door opens, and Aurora enters, fresh and beautiful as ever.

My feelings are too much for me. I fling away my hat. I catch Aurora to my bosom, and gazing upwards with a vision dimmed with tears of joy, find that Aurora's mamma has accompanied her child, and that she seems to be wondering what the deuce I am doing!

--------0--------

CHAPTER XXII.

IN WHICH THE MAJOR GOES FOR A GODFATHER.

AN accident has recalled the fact to my mind that my fag at old Merchant Taylors' is still alive, and appears to be getting on pretty middling.

The fellow's name, by a curious chance, was Penniwate, and in the old Merchant Taylors' days it was my habit to make merry over the fact that Penniwate waited on Penny!

I have frequently laughed at this jest (my own) myself. P.W. did not laugh much, if I remember He was a heavy kind of boy, and fat. He made a good warming-pan on sharp frosty nights.

To-day, glancing through the "Times" (it is odd my letter suggesting a site for the Needle is not in to-day, but doubtless it will appear to-morrow—I presume there is occasionally a press of correspondence), I observe a person of the name of Penniwate subscribing a largish sum to a charity.

Ebenezer Penniwate! That *must* be my old fag And here is his business address, Bleeding Hart Yard. The very place for a charitably disposed person to live in. Naturally, under the circumstances, his heart would bleed for the sufferings of his fellow-creatures.

Why should it not bleed for the twins? It shall!

This is really a remarkably happy thought of mine! Penniwate will feel honoured by my calling on him. Hang me! I shouldn't wonder if the fellow feels a little frightened, to begin with, when he first hears my name. I rather fancy I should in his place.

Lord, how I used to give it to that fellow! I think I recollect how knotted towels and buckle-ends of straps were liberally applied to a tightened surface. I toasted him, too, if I remember rightly, inside the high fire-screen; and at another time stood him, in his night-shirt, in the snow to sing " Hot Codlins," and he did the sneezing so awfully lifelike, we encored him.

Decidedly he should be Godfather to these two poor boys! He will be glad of the chance, proud of the honour. I'll go and see him at once.

I walk to the station, I take a third return upon principle, because the Company have suppressed the second class in the hope of forcing me to ride first. I will *not* ride first, as I mentioned before, on principle. The third has a confoundedly hard seat, and the people who ride with me are confoundedly objectionable; but I have my principle, and to my principle I stick.

One of our local gentry passes by whilst I am looking out of the carriage window, and I nod to him. He rather jumps when he sees where I am, but I smile blandly, and I say,

" You are surprised that I should ride third? "

He says, " Yes, I am."

I say, " I do it on principle."

He says, " But the other's only threepence-halfpenny more on the double journey."

I smile. " Yes, but I do it on principle."

He says, " You must be a stupid fool to make yourself jolly uncomfortable to save threepence-halfpenny."

" Confound you, sir ! " I say. " Don't you understand——"

But he has gone, and I have to content myself with explaining the facts of the case to an old woman with a bundle on the opposite seat. She says,

" Quite right too, sir. If you can't afford it, why should you ? Third's good enough for the likes of me and you, sure—ly."

*   *   *   *   *   *

You my possibly never have visited Bleeding Hart Yard. Had Penniwate not lived there, I am not quite sure that I should have visited it myself.

They say that it is going to be pulled down. Possibly Penniwate's premises may tumble down of their own accord before then. They at present appear to be in a tottering condition, and only want a strong gale of wind, or a good shove, to topple them over into the road.

Poor Penniwate is, after all, perhaps, not getting on quite as well as I had at first supposed.

I have heard of such things as people, even when on the eve of bankruptcy, subscribing to popular charities, by way of advertisement, to make other people think

they are all right.   Possibly I have done wrong in
selecting Penniwate as a Godfather.

The house is dreadfully dirty, and the passage
blocked up by empty boxes and other lumber.   Evidently Penniwate's business is on its last legs, or worse
than that even—on crutches.   I enter a dimly-lighted
office, which smells damp and mouldy, and ask for my
ancient fag.   "Is he in?"

"I'll go and see, sir," says a weak-eyed young man,
who comes and blinks at me furtively.

I can understand Penniwate's position.   Afraid of
duns.   Don't know whether he is at home or not.

"Shall I take up your name, sir?"

"Tell him Major Penny desires to see him."

"Penny what, sir?"

"Penny nothing.   Major Penny!"

"Oh, I beg pardon, sir; I thought it sounded as if
there was something short."

What does he mean by that? I am half inclined to
think he means impertinence, but I won't go into it.
To be sure, Penny weight—Short weight.   I'll speak
to P.W. about this when I see him.

*   *   *   *   *   *

The boy is a deuce of a long while gone.   A profound silence prevails in the place of business.   Not
a soul comes in to buy anything.

Deadly-lively job this of P W's, it strikes me.

I have been waiting over half an hour.   I hammer
on the counter.   A grey-headed man comes to speak
to me.   He wants to know what I want.   I tell him.

He says he knows nothing of it, but he supposes the boy passed my name up the pipe.

Is it dignified for a Major, who has led forces on the ensanguined field of battle, to have his name and title passed up a pipe? This is a nice point. I might almost write to the editor of the "Times" to ask his opinion on the subject.

Waiting.

---o---

CHAPTER XXIII.

IN WHICH THE MAJOR LANDS A GODFATHER.

THE grey-headed man proposes passing my name up the pipe again to make sure. Confound him and his pipe! But I suppose he means no offence, so I mention my name to him.

He says, "What?"

I say, "Major Penny."

He says, "Penniwate, I suppose?"

I say, "Certainly not. Penny."

He repeats, "Not Penny. No; I said Penniwate. Connection of the guv'nor, I suppose?"

"No, sir," I reply, naturally indignant, "no connection. Don't want to be. My name is simply Penny. P—E—N—N—Y. Will you please say I have waited a long while?"

The grey-headed man retires to a corner, and I hear a faint whisper to this effect: "Here's Penny, and he says he won't wait."

Then I hear a voice in the pipe using bad language, and asking, "Who's playing the fool?"

Explanations ensue between the man this end and Penniwate himself at the other, and, at last, word comes down that I am to go upstairs.

I do so; but I somehow don't feel quite so much in the humour for the interview as I did at first. I have indeed half a mind to throw the whole thing up, and go home.

However, I go upstairs. I knock at a door indicated.

"Come in!" cries a voice inside. There is nothing at all encouraging—or, indeed, I may say, respectful —about the tone of the voice; but I think it, perhaps, best to go in, as I have come on purpose.

There is, however, a difficulty about opening the door, for the handle of which I search upon the wrong side, to begin with. Whilst still searching, I hear bad language within the room.

Even now I have a good mind to give up the god-father notion, and go away. However, I don't do that; I go on looking for the door-handle.

"Bother you!" says the voice. But it is more than bother, if the truth must be told. "Why don't you come in?"

I am almost in pitch darkness out here, and am still groping wildly for the door-handle. It would seem so absurd to give it up and go away, but I don't see anything else for it, unless the person inside chooses to offer some assistance. He has—just when I was leaning against the door, too—and I go in with a run, my hat going in advance.

"The handle's off the outside," he says. "Couldn't you find that out, without such a jolly lot of fumbling?" (only he doesn't exactly say jolly).

I ignore the expletives, and say, "I desire to speak to Mr. Penniwate."

"Well, speak, can't you?" says the person confronting me; "you've been long enough about it."

I look at him—I look at him very hard. Is it possible that this is my Penniwate? He used to be my junior—several years my junior, but he appears to have grown so old. He positively has not a hair on his head.

"You—you are the same that was at Merchant Taylors', aren't you?" I ask—"at school, I mean, thirty years ago?"

He pauses for a moment to think. "Yes," he replies, slowly, "I was at school there. What of it?

The bills were paid, I believe. Nobody owes any-thing on my account that I know of; and if they do, you ought to have sent in your claim sooner."

I can scarcely forbear from a smile. "Don't you know me?" (I pause here to think whether he had a nickname. To be sure he had. We gave him one, after that "Hot Codlins" business.) "Don't you know me, Eben-sneezer?"

The truth appears to dawn upon him gradually.

"You're old Penny!" he cries.

Hang "*old* Penny!" But stay, old is a kind of term of endearment among boys. "To be sure I am," I say.

There is a short pause.

"What a beast I used to think you!" he says, in a dreamy tone. "You've got to be very podgy."

Hang "podgy!" I don't like this at all. "You've got awfully thin on top," I retort. "Indeed, thin is hardly the word."

There is another pause.

"Why did you come here?" he asks.

"I'll tell you," I reply. "You're a bachelor—don't speak!—I know you are by the look of you. I—I am the uncle of two boys; in point of fact, twin boys. I want a Godfather for them. I saw your name in the paper this morning. I recognized it. A flood of pleasant memories rushed through my mind. I said, 'I will go and see him this very day.' I did. Here I am!"

One more of those pauses.

"You want me to be the twins' Godfather?" he says.

"That is just what I do want."

"What are the duties of a Godfather?" he asks, in

the same dreamy tone he used before, and I noticed his eyes wander towards an open cheque-book on the table.

Awfully happy thought! Duties? Duties in three figures. But it will be best not to startle him too much at first.

The Appeal.

"Really and truly," I say, "beyond the mugs—or shall we say spoons and forks, or mugs and spoons and forks?—I don't think there are any duties particularly insisted on."

"Oh!" he says, "all right; I'll be their Godfather. Good day to you!"

*   *   *   *   *   *

The last part of our interview was a trifle abrupt, it seemed to me, but two or three people seemed to be shouting up the pipe as I tried to explain to him where

I lived, and what train he ought to catch to be in time
for the christening.

The day has arrived. I have written in the meanwhile to P W., so that there could be no mistake. He
ought to be here by eleven sharp, and then we shall
have plenty of time.

The Outrage.

We have offered him a bed. He might as well sleep
here. It will be rather a nuisance, perhaps; but then,
as he is to be Godfather, and with that cheque-book—
I believe, too, he really is *not* so very badly off.

Eleven thirty-five. No signs of him. Twelve.
Still no signs, and the ceremony is fixed for half-
past twelve!

Twelve fifteen. A parcel come by rail. What on
earth is this?

My blood boils. I can hardly trust myself to speak,
but I must.

Here is a note. He sends two mugs, and two forks, and two spoons, but he doesn't feel equal to the rest of the duties.

Well! do you say? There are, anyhow, two mugs, two forks, and two spoons to the good. Is that what you were pleased to remark? Look here! The mugs are earthenware—the forks and spoons of wood!!

----o----

CHAPTER XXIV

IN WHICH THERE IS VERY NEARLY A MISTAKE IN THE CEREMONY.

I HAVE settled on the names.

As I intend that the twins themselves shall devote their lives to the upholding of the honour and glory of Old England—one in the army and the other in the navy—I have decided on calling the first twin Alexander, and the second Horatio.

In consequence of Rosabel and Aurora's mamma having kindly offered to act as Godmother to Alexander, in deference to a wish she has expressed it is my intention to add Montgomery as a second name; whilst, with respect to Horatio, the fact that my old friend Captain Pincher has promised to do the needful in his case (inclusive of a mug of elegant

9—2

design), we shall be compelled to couple Horatio with
Pincher. It seems a pity, but it can't very well be
helped ; and, somehow, Pincher doesn't seem to be
aware what a beast of a name he has got.

Several times I have been on the point of breaking
it gently to Pincher that it won't do, but consideration
for Pincher's feelings has caused me to refrain. Besides,
as though Pincher's male parent had not done him
deadly wrong enough by giving him such a surname,
he has added insult to injury by calling him Aminadab.
If I reject one, I must take the other, or quarrel with
Pincher for life.

Taking a stroll up the high road the evening before
the ceremony, I meet Pincher coming at a deuce of a
pace round a corner, and panting for breath.

"Hallo! Captain," I say, "what's the matter?"

Pincher takes off his hat, and dabs at his forehead
with his pocket-handkerchief. "Matter!" he gasps ;
"everything's the matter. It's not come! What
the deuce is to be done?"

"The—the mug?" I say, suddenly interested.

"Yes. I've telegraphed for it, and I'm on my way
down to the station again to make further inquiry."

"That's right," I say, with much earnestness ; "stick
to them. Put up with none of their nonsense!"

Pincher dabs at his forehead once more, crushes
down his hat, and scuds away up the hill as fast as his
poor old legs will carry him.

It is really an awfully funny sight, is Pincher's back
view, under these circumstances. I confess I cannot
refrain from a smile. Indeed, I sit down on a low wall
and roar.

The Christening.

Then the thought occurs to me, "Supposing, after all, the mug is really lost?   I don't see much fun in that."

*   *   *   *   *   *

Evidently the twins are impressed with the importance of the ceremony in store for them.

They have scarcely slept a wink all night. No more has anybody else ; but that, apparently, does not signify to the twins.

Mrs. Montgomery has seen them early this morning, and says that they are feverish, and must be kept very warm. Unfortunately, it is an awfully bleak day, with an east wind like a knife. I wonder whether it is customary to have the chill taken off the water in the font under such circumstances?   I'll ask the clerk.

By the time we ought to start, neither Pincher nor his mug have put in an appearance. Perhaps, however, he intends to meet us at the church. The ladies are all ready and waiting. We have glasses of wine and biscuits, and set forth.

Mrs. Montgomery heads the procession.

Next in order follow Rosabel and Aurora, each carrying a twin.

Then come Maud and Beatrix (sisters of Rosabel and Aurora), who say "Ketchetty!" to the twins over Rosabel and Aurora's shoulders.

After them come Bathsheba, Cassandra, and Ursula, and—

I, Major Penny, bring up the rear!

A mongrel dog, of an irreverent nature, runs behind and barks. I call to it to "Get out," but it won't ;

and I ultimately decide upon ignoring its presence, and the procession continues.

At the turn of the road we find an imbecile native of these parts seated on a gate.

When he sees us he appears to be amused. He says, "Lookee at 'un droivin' t' goslin's to t' market!" and as I take no notice of him, continues to indulge in similar ribaldries as long as we are in sight.

As we approach the church, I lead the procession with Mrs. Montgomery, so as to be able to make a few preliminary arrangements of a necessary character.

An ancient female, apparently very short-sighted, meets us in the porch and drops a curtsey.

"It's your turn next, deary," she says, with a smile of great affability; "and after you a christening."

The ancient female seems to mean some kind of joke by this—only I don't quite see it.

"We are the christening," I observe, "unless there are two."

"Two!" repeats the ancient female, who, by the way, seems to be rather hard of hearing as well as dim of sight. "Yes, deary, they're twins, but it's quite exceptional."

"Confound you!" I exclaim, "don't you know we want to be the christen—— I mean—confound you! —we're the christening——"

"All right, deary, there's no occasion to call so loud. You're most old enough to have got a name, sir, I should think. But I understand your fun: the lady wants to change hers. So you shall, deary. It's your turn next."

This old woman is intolerable. What is to be done

with her? She appears to have told somebody, who has told somebody else, that we are a wedding——

On looking again, I observe the clergyman in the distance (who happens to be a stranger to me, doing duty for our curate, away on a holiday), appearing very impatient, and wondering why we don't come forward.

Presently the clerk begins beckoning to me, and I think it best to go up and explain.

"Come, come, my dear sir," says the strange clergyman, "you'll be too late directly. Do make haste, if you want to be married."

"The fact is," I reply, "I don't want to be married."

"Good gracious!" says the strange clergyman. "I trust that the lady has not——"

"No, no," I hasten to assure him, "we're not the marriage—we're the christening."

"What made you say you wanted to be married, then?" says the strange clergyman, evidently very angry. "A joke of this kind—you will excuse my telling you, sir—is ill-timed and ill-placed in this sacred edifice."

I feel I am getting very hot and very red. I should like to knock the strange clergyman over backwards among the hassocks, but I refrain, and retire somewhat ignominiously, as it seems to me.

Meanwhile the wedding party don't show up. No more does Pincher—with the mug. Confound Pincher! I shan't forgive this very readily.

At length, after a longish wait, the strange clergyman determines on taking our case first, and, after a little awkwardness, owing to the clerk in the confusion having opened his book for him at the funeral service, the ceremony begins.

I suppose it is not very long, but the twins are howling so loudly, I am not sure what is being said. Presently, however, I am asked for the twins' names, and have to hand up a twin.

Owing to more confusion, somebody hands me the wrong twin first, and that puts me out again so much that, for the life of me, I can think of nothing in the way of a name for him but Pincher.

It is not likely that I shall give him that one after what has occurred, and so in desperation I say "John!" and Twin No. 1 is so christened amidst general consternation.

I am then called upon for the name of No. 2 Twin, and have to hand him to the strange clergyman across the font, into which I as nearly as possible drop him; and, owing to my memory being at the time a perfect blank, No. 2 is called Thomas, to save time.

This is deuced awkward, but I don't see how it can be helped now.

And, now it is all over, here is Pincher—without the mug!

CHAPTER XXV

IN WHICH IT IS A QUESTION OF THE TWINS' TEETH.

I SHOULD feel extremely obliged to the reader if she (these chapters were never intended for the perusal of male persons) would kindly imagine that time has rolled on, and that the twins are some months older.

    ✷   ✷   *   *   ✷   *

N.B.—The rolling on of time and the growth of twins are indicated by these stars.

    ✷   ✷   *   *   *

I have made it up with Pincher. I have found that Pincher was not altogether to blame in not turning up in time at the ceremony. The sufferings, mental and physical, endured by Pincher upon the day of the ceremony, with regard to the mug, would appear to have been intense.

The number of times those poor old legs of his carried Pincher over the hill to the station and back again, to meet every train, you would hardly credit.

That his exertions were eventually crowned with success, I hasten to testify. The mug did come at last, and so indeed, did, a second mug also, which, in sheer desperation, Pincher had telegraphed for, when he thought there was no chance of the original mug turning up.

Since then there have been County Court actions relative to the mug in question, and cross actions, from which serious unpleasantness has resulted. To speak of mugs since then, in Pincher's presence, is to bring about ebullitions of temper best avoided.

Since the ceremony, I regret to say, the twins have not been at all well. The abnormal wolfishness of the twins' appetites has largely subsided. They have had what Mrs. Montgomery describes as "nasty little rashes." They have had coughs and colds, and spasmodic twitchings of an alarming character, and Mrs. Montgomery says it's "all the teeth."

It would appear that the twins are backward in their teething, and that the rashes, coughs, colds, and spasmodic twitchings are the natural results of this backwardness.

I say, "Oughtn't something to be done?" and Mrs. Montgomery produces a teething mixture composed of tincture of cinnamon and powdered chalk, and we administer it according to the written instructions, at the rate of two teaspoonfuls per twin three times per diem, but it doesn't seem to do any particular good.

Can it be possible, I ask myself, that Mrs. Montgomery is wrong respecting the twins' ailment? Fortunately, I have a work I have recently purchased treating of infants' ailments, and I look up "Teething" in the index.

The book says, "The period when the teeth may be expected is indicated by an increased irritability of the infant."

To judge by these indications, this would seem to be the period—only that, to the best of my recollection, the twins have always been rather irritable. Are they more so now than usual?

As yet, as there are none of the signs of the teeth coming through the gums, indicated in the work of reference, I cannot quite make up my mind whether or not Mrs. Montgomery is not labouring under a delusion. One reason for my having my doubts respecting Mrs. M.'s knowledge is, that I strongly suspect her of fixing the name of the complaint after finding the recipe, instead of first settling what the complaint is. Mrs. Montgomery, as a mother of four, however, being the only one of the eleven concerned with any practical knowledge on the subject of infant ailments, Bathsheba, Cassandra, Ursula, Rosabel, Aurora, Beatrix, Maud, the twins, and I, are compelled to bow to her decision, and respectively buy, mix, administer, or swallow, as the case may be, the medicines prescribed.

A prey to varied emotions, I go over the hill for a constitutional, and accidentally meet my old friend Dr. Bloggs—Bloggs of ours—who is quartered at the market town.

This is, it seems to me, a capital opportunity of getting an opinion on the case, and I artfully lure Bloggs in the direction of my house, and insist on his coming in and having a glass of sherry and a biscuit.

With the sherry and the biscuit I, with more artfulness, produce a twin—the most irritable one—and ask him what he thinks of it.

I have since had reason to believe that Bloggs has not given much attention to the ailments of infancy, and is better at cutting off legs or sewing wounds up with wire.

He says, "What's that?"

I reply, "My nephew—a fine little fellow, don't you think? One of two—twins."

Bloggs—his joke.

He says, "Looks unwholesome, don't he?"

I hardly like this way of putting it, but I don't think Bloggs means any harm. He has a rough way with him, that is all.

I say, "I think he is out of sorts just now—I am told he is teething. But, I suppose, as soon as he cuts his teeth——"

"That doesn't follow," says Bloggs. "There are several diseases that teething gives rise to—as, for instance, convulsions, water on the brain, rickets, and remittent fevers. He might be sickening for one of them—perhaps the lot."

I gasp as he enumerates these horrors, and drink off half a glass of sherry to steady my nerves.

"I—I hope it won't be so serious as all that!" I say ; "but what disturbs me most is that I can't help thinking it's a back tooth he is going to cut first. If that's the case, what would you advise ?"

"If that *is* the case," says Bloggs, "I should be inclined to have it out right off. I don't see what else could be done." And with this Bloggs puts on his hat, and prepares to take his departure.

Confound Bloggs! I'm sorry now I wasted the sherry and biscuits on him. I remember, in my time, the fellow was a confirmed practical joker. Yet, again, he seemed in earnest. What ought I to do?

I have it. I'll go and see my friend Bowden, and take the twins with me.

When I say I will take the twins, I mean I will accompany some member of my household, who will carry the twins—or, more properly speaking, perhaps two members of my household, who will carry a twin each—say Rosabel and Aurora.

Although not, strictly speaking, members of my household, Mrs. Montgomery and her two other daughters, Beatrix and Maud, are pretty frequently with us, and, hearing what I propose, think it will be a capital opportunity to go up to town and do a little shopping.

The Girls, acquainted with this project, also intimate a desire to shop, and think they cannot do better than join the party.

This is not, strictly speaking, quite what I desired, but I don't know exactly how to refuse, so we all start together, and I pay the nine fares.

———o———

CHAPTER XXVI.

IN WHICH THE TWINS CAUSE MORE ANXIETY.

MY friend Bowden has a first floor in Charles Street, St. James's, of reasonable dimensions ; but, as we approach it, I have an uneasy suspicion that we shall make rather a crowd in his drawing-room.

As this reflection occurs to me, I look up and observe my friend Bowden at the window, and wonder whether he thinks I'm bringing him a lady's school.

Under these circumstances, therefore, I induce six of the party to go and eat buns at a neighbouring baker's, and, accompanied by Aurora and Rosabel, consult my friend Bowden about the twins' teeth. He is not of opinion that the back teeth will come first ; on the contrary, he gives the preference to the central incisors, and is of opinion that after them we may expect the lateral incisors, and then not be surprised to see some of the canines. In the meanwhile, he thinks the twins appear to be getting on as well as can be expected, and is not in favour of an operation being performed just yet awhile on either of them.

After which he insists upon Rosabel, Aurora, and I taking a glass of his particular port, and just half a glass each afterwards, and the time passes quite pleasantly until a couple of patients arrive, and we all have a kind of guilty consciousness of the mamma, and the

Poof!

Girls, and Beatrix, and Maud languishing round the corner on dry buns.

I don't know how it is, but few things in life seem to me much more enjoyable than visiting your Dentist when it is not your own tooth that is to be operated on.

The six at the Pastrycook's are waiting for us, and glad we have come. There are only the buns to pay for, and we may start.

After this the ladies do a little shopping, and I wait outside the shops, and then we go to the " Criterion,"

and have a little lunch, and take the train home. It
is not, perhaps, a cheap trip this, but it is a very
pleasant one. The twins are more than usually irritable. That is all there is to complain of.

*   *   *   *   *   *

The twins go on that night in a way we are unused
to, even in them.

What is to be done?

In the morning Mrs. Montgomery (she and her two
other daughters stayed here last night—it was so late
for them to go home—and I slept on the parlour sofa)
knocks at the parlour door, and beseeches me to lose
no time, but run for the Doctor.

I run with all my might, and come full butt against
Pincher round a corner. I tell Pincher what a state of
mind I am in, and we run together. We bring back
the best of the two local Doctors, and he gives the
twins something soothing, and leaves them apparently

easier in their minds, but he says it will be a good job when it is all over.

We think so too, and seek our couches that night, worn and weary, at an earlier hour than usual. According to my friend Bowden, the twins' teeth were not far off; but the local Doctor says it may be weeks, and there is no telling which twin will survive. Certainly not both.

*   *   *   *   *   *

Another day has dawned. A report reaches me that the twins are sitting up in their little cot, radiant as sunshine. Presently I go to the nursery, and pass my finger gently into Twin No. 1's mouth.

He bites it.

I don't give No. 2 a chance, but I grapple with him and examine his jaw.

Both twins have cut their central incisors!

"He's cut 'em."

CHAPTER XXVII.

IN WHICH SOMEBODY DOES SOMETHING SILLY.

THIS has really not been at all a pleasant morning. The local tradesmen's quarterly bills have just come in, and I find them considerably larger than usual.

I observe, in going into details, that the physic for the twins is the principal item in the local Doctor's account. Casting my eye over the Grocer's account, I perceive that the twins' "foods" come to money. Yet I am inclined to think that our increase of expenditure may also, to some extent, be attributed to other causes. When I casually mention that I have recently learnt that it is Aurora's opinion that the best fresh butter, and the best fresh butter alone, is absolutely necessary for all culinary purposes, I trust that the sagacious reader will find a wink to be equal to a nod.

In addition to the circumstance above alluded to, I may, I trust, be pardoned if I state what might almost appear like a truism, namely, that although possibly upon occasion what was enough for one has been found to be enough for two, what was enough for Dawkins does not entirely suffice for five. I allude to the fact that, of late, Mrs. Montgomery and her two other daughters pretty well live here.

In the character of host, I am willing to allow that a hearty appreciation of the viands decking my humble board is what I desire to see, and it is, possibly,

almost ungentlemanly—unmanly even, I may say—
to count up what it costs to support these four young
and lovely girls and their mamma; yet, you know, as
I have to pay——

With regard to the other Girls—the old original
ones—I notice, with some uneasiness, that they are
not altogether what they used to be. To some extent
the air of contentment which was one of their chief
characteristics in times gone by exists no longer. The
advent of the military, which, it may be recollected, I
foresaw would bring trouble to our hitherto happy
home, has wrought havoc and desolation.

A flightiness hitherto undreamt of has taken possession of the Girls, and the stock-in-trade of the chief
Linendraper at the neighbouring market town no
longer suffices for their wants. Journeys to town for
the purpose of shopping are of frequent occurrence,
and Aurora, Rosabel, Beatrix, Maud, and their mamma go shopping too, and have their purchases put
down in the Girls' bills.

Upon my venturing to remonstrate — attempts at
the assertion of my authority have not recently been
successful enough to warrant frequent repetition—the
Girls' conduct is most extraordinary.

"One might as well be an oyster at once, as live in
this stupid humdrum hole," exclaims Bathsheba, "and
I, for one, will endure it no longer!"

    *   *   *   *   *   *

Although I have most effectually sent the bold private soldiers to the right about, I find my house con-

stantly besieged by the officers from the neighbouring
town, who ride over, lunch, and dine, and take tea
with us any number of times a week, and occasionally
stay to supper. To say that their spurs have ruined
all my chair-legs and frayed my best drawing-room
carpet, would be to say nothing; and, indeed, perhaps
I ought not to mention it here.

Cassandra says; "Perhaps some day they may no
longer annoy you by their presence."

I think that is more than probable. I expect they
will change their quarters soon, and I shan't be sorry.

Bless me!

A sudden light has broken in upon me, and I am
absolutely dazzled. The Girls actually — at their
time of life, too! and especially Bathsheba, at her
time of life—labour under the impression that these
young fellows come here rasping my chair-legs on
account of—— Upon my word of honour, it is too
ridiculous!

*   *   *   *   *   *

I am, at this moment, in my *sanctum sanctorum*,
grappling with the Butcher's bill, when there comes a
soft tap at the door. Probably Aurora, to consult me
about to-day's dinner. In that case, I must be firm
with her. Even if she calls me a Cross Old Thing, I
must still be steadfast to my purpose. This reckless
extravagance can no longer continue.

"Come in!"

It is Aurora's mamma. "Oh, Major, I hope I am
not disturbing you," she says; "but I do so much
want to have a few moments' serious talk with you

about—you, however, no doubt, know what I would say."

I reply that, if the truth must be told, I have not the remotest notion.

She seems surprised at this, and says, "In that case I cannot be too explicit. In these cases one never can."

I bow. What's coming, I wonder?

"Major," she says, "I of course speak on behalf of my children. That you had long ago won the respect, the esteem—nay, why should I not say the love and affection?—of all, can be no secret to you, and I will not, I cannot deny that in whatever direction your preference may lie, there will always be a certain amount of disappointment, which, however, you must not, nay, you should not, permit to influence your choice."

"You'll excuse me, Mrs. Montgomery," I observe, "but what in the name of goodness do you mean?"

"I simply mean," says Mrs. Montgomery, "that as a mother I cannot permit this distracting uncertainty any longer to continue, and I must insist on your saying which it is."

"Good gracious me, ma'am!" I gasp out, "if any member of your accomplished and amiable family labours under the idea that I am going to propose to her, she is, I may say, utterly mistaken. If—if I ever intended to do such a thing, I—I should select some one more of my own age—some one—I trust you understand me."

"Oh, Major," says Mrs. Montgomery, "I do now; but until this moment I had not the faintest suspicion of the real state of your feelings. I cannot, it is true, give you in return a girl's first love, for I will not deny that one, who is now no more, I loved deeply and devotedly——"

"Confound it, ma'am!" I cry out, "this is getting right down ridiculous. You must be a stupid old fool!"

✳   ✳   ✳   ✳   ✳   ✳

CHAPTER XXVIII.

IN WHICH TWOPENNY TURNS UP.

THERE have been scenes! Several scenes! Everything is at an end every way. Everybody is going. Everybody is packing up. Every one has denounced me. It would appear that I ought to be ashamed of myself: I am not sure I am not.

Aurora and Rosabel's little luggage stands in the hall; the carrier's cart will fetch it presently. They have clung to the Girls and wept, but they say 't is better thus. The Girls say that this is no longer a home for them either. They themselves appear to be only waiting for the men with the spurs to turn up and carry them off. Presently the twins and I will be alone in our glory.

In the midst of all this a shabby stranger arrives, with a single knock.   I open the door to him, and he hands me a thumb-marked, crumpled envelope, containing a note to this effect :

"SIR,—Excuse the liberty I take in addressing you, but want must plead as my excuse. If you can oblige me with the loan of a pound or fifteen shillings until the end of the week, when I expect to sell some shares in a public company, I should feel obliged.

"Your affectionate brother-in-law,

"PERCY TWOPENNY.

"P.S.—Perhaps you would like to buy some of the shares yourself. My friend, whom you can trust with the money, has them with him. Please make it a pound if possible."

This, then, is the father of the Twins !!!

*   *   *   *   *   *

The man has gone, and — did not kick him. Neither did I send the-money or buy the shares.

*   *   *   *   *   *

Three days have elapsed since Rosabel and Aurora quitted my house. The Girls have cried almost incessantly. We are all very wretched. I almost wish some of those young fellows with the spurs would turn up again, if only for a change.

But they don't. The Girls seem to think this singular.

At last one does turn up—not, however, one of the most regular of our visitors; but I welcome him cordially, and ask after the four regular ones, Bragshaw, Bagshaw, Ragshaw, and Wagshaw (these names will do as well as any others). My visitor looks knowing. He supposes they're more agreeably engaged. By the way, they are all *engaged*. Didn't I know?

"Engaged! to whom?" I ask.

"Go on," he says. "Why, it was you brought it all about. They told me so. They're nice girls, ain't they? Not much tin, but deuced nice."

"D—d—do you mean the Miss Montgomerys?" I stammer.

He does! How am I to break this to those poor, wretched, miserable, unhappy Girls?

*   *   *   *   *   *

Three weeks have elapsed. It has been broken to those poor, wretched, miserable, unhappy Girls, and they are bad! Just at present they talk of emigrating, or going out to the seat of war as hospital nurses. Just at present I don't think it is any particular good trying to conciliate them.

They say the Montgomery girls are deceitful cats.

*   *   *   *   *   *

Of course I only ask out of sheer curiosity, but I wonder whether either Rosabel, Aurora, Beatrix, or

Maud really did entertain any, and, in that case, whether they wanted to make sure before settling with the young fellows with the spurs.

     *   *   *   *   *   *

The shabby man again, and another rather shabbier —Twopenny, the father of the twins.

Both appear to be the worse for liquor. Twopenny says he is the twins' legal protector, and wants to take them away with him. I ask, Where? He says, the workhouse, in which it is his intention to end his days.

I say, "Look here, Twopenny, this sort of thing won't do, you know. Don't you come here trying on this sort of thing any more, because it won't do."

He says (with a hiccup), "Give me my children. It is but right that I should have them. Am I not their sole surviving parent?"

His friend adds, "Certainly, old boy. Don't you stand none of his nonsense."

I do not, however, give Twopenny his twins, as desired, but I give him a trifle in silver instead, and he goes away in a happier frame of mind, with another hiccup.

Will he come back again, though?

I expect he will.

     *   *   *   *   *   *

Three months have elapsed. The poor blighted Girls are still living beneath my roof.

So are the twins.

Twopenny sends for them at intervals, dating his letters from various casual wards, hospitals, and police stations, but they are still with me.

The Montgomery girls are married.

My solicitor tells me Mrs. Montgomery has no case, but I must personally defend the action. He says that in these breach of promise businesses the man always gets awfully guyed, but I mustn't mind that. I am trying not to mind much. I am trying to look forward to the guying with indifference, and am trying to pretend I shall rather enjoy it.

*　　*　　*　　*　　*　　*

Three years have elapsed.

The Girls have not emigrated as yet. A new Curate has come down to our parish. We have him in to tea pretty frequently. He has a taste for music, and is fond of water-colour painting ; he also is a collector, in a small way, of old china. We are not quite sure in which direction he may indicate a preference, but at present I see no reason why I should offer any opposition.

He is a man of superior attainments, and has a great deal of shrewd common sense. I read him all my letters to the editor of the " Times," and he is of opinion that it is a shame they are not inserted.

It is over a year since I last saw anything of Twopenny. This may be a good sign. I shan't advertise for him. He may turn up again, and he mayn't. There's an amount of uncertainty about it, it is true, which is in a way worrying, but I think I prefer the uncertainty to Twopenny as a present and palpable fact.

I have pretty well got over the recollections of my sufferings in that confounded law court; pretty nearly, but not quite.

There are other recollections, too, associated with the name of Montgomery, not quite so easily got over, perhaps.

But I don't mention this before the Girls.

I should feel obliged if you too would not mention this before the Girls.

The twins have been short-coated some time now.

TERMINATION OF THE TWINS.